INNOCENT BLOOD

Books by Michael Lister

(John Jordan novels)
Power in the Blood
Blood of the Lamb
Flesh and Blood
The Body and the Blood
Blood Sacrifice
Rivers to Blood
Innocent Blood
Blood Money

(Jimmy "Soldier" Riley novels)
The Big Goodbye
The Big Beyond
The Big Hello
The Big Bout

(Short Story Collections)
North Florida Noir
Florida Heat Wave
Delta Blues
Another Quiet Night in Desparation

(Remington James novels)
Double Exposure
Separation Anxiety

(Merrick McKnight novels)
Thunder Beach
A Certain Retribution

(Sam Michaels and Daniel Davis Series)
Burnt Offerings
Separation Anxiety

(The Meaning Series)
Finding the Way Again
Meaning Every Moment
The Meaning of Life in Movies
The Meaning of Life

(Love Stories)
Carrie's Gift

Innocent Blood

a John Jordan Mystery

by Michael Lister

Special Introduction by
Michael Connelly

Pulpwood Press

This is a work of fiction. Any similarities to people or places, living or dead, is purely coincidental.

Inquiries should be addressed to:
Pulpwood Press
P.O. Box 35038
Panama City, FL 32412

Lister, Michael.
Innocent Blood / Michael
Lister.
-----1st ed.
p. cm.

ISBN: 978-1-888146-49-3 Hardcover

ISBN: 978-1-888146-50-9 Paperback

Book Design by Adam Ake

Printed in the United States

1 3 5 7 9 10 8 6 4 2

First Edition

For

For those I first encountered and who quickly became family upon my arrival in Atlanta:

The Paulks: LaDonna, Don, Clariece, Earl, Norma, and DE; Rick Howington, Randy Renfroe, Dana Harris, Deanna Harris, Richard Gaydos, Jeff Moore, Lance Young, Arie Rumph, Richie Haynes, Keith Philips, Dawn Brewer, Rick and Cheryl Busby, Adrian Bailey, Lonnie Holloway, Ken and Janice McFarland, Greg and Cindy Hall, Russ Butcher, Bob Blackwood, Dan Rhodes, Pete Aycock, Jim Oborne, Duane Swilley, Tricia Weeks, Chip Wood, Jack Hammonds, Laura Gunter, Pam Palmer, Amy Palmer, Sue Skipper, Cheryl McGuire, John and Dottie Bridges, George Anthony, Don Ross, John and Derinda Hembree, Jeff and Lisa Gabriel, Vicki Howington, Rebecca Howington, Barry Smith, Don Kreglewicz, Lesley Ferguson, Dana Blackwood, Roger Foat, Cassius Turner, Kirby Clements, James Powers, Lynn Mays, Dawn Bagwell, Hannah Holmes, Suzanne Mays, Angie Martin, JulieMartin, Tonya Oborne, Bobby Brewer, Mike Stanborough, Rob Stanborough, Chip Poole, Teresa Bridges Lucas, Karl Horstmann, Gino Zalunardo, Misty Stephens, JohnWiese, Jim and Dee Felt, Pedro Torres, Mike and Mozelle Cole, Gary Moore, Jerry Moore, Jon and Janice Stallings, Benny and Marla Grizzell, Raye Varney, David Pulaski, Matt Lucas, Rhonda Price, Teri Legg, Kristin Lee, Teresa Cozart, Dan Shives, Cheryl Blalock, Greg Maxwell, Dean Wild, Michael Yates, Michelle Gonzales, Randy Puckett, Sally Nicholson, Bubba and Kathi Wilson, Bob Hunter, Barry Smith.

And for Tony and Kim Bolton for making the introduction.

Special thanks to

Dawn Lister, Jill Mueller,
Adam Ake, Samuel Lourcey,
Lou Columbus, LaDonna Paulk Diaz,
Randy Renfroe, Don and Clariece Paulk,
and Michael Connelly

INTRODUCTION
by Michael Connelly

The reading of a novel is a mysterious and sacred thing. A solely internal process, it relies totally on one's empathy, the ability to connect with another being – the story's protagonist. To me it's like thumbing a ride and getting into a car with a stranger behind the wheel. Except this driver doesn't ask where you're headed because you are going wherever he goes. So you head off and over time you get to know the driver. You can't help it. You learn all about him as he drives. You pick up little stories, little moments of character. And yet he won't tell you where he's taking you. But that's okay because not knowing the destination is the key to a good ride. And if you are lucky the conversation and the scenery along the way is equally as interesting as the final destination.

It is a massive investment of time and creative energy to read a novel. You have to build characters in your imagination, even if they're villains and you don't like them. You create landscapes and emotions. It's all very risky. Because the emotions are real even if the story isn't. A sacred bond develops between the reader and the stranger behind the wheel.

All of that is why you are in for a great ride with this book and why the following pages hold such a treat. If you are like me you've already invested heavily in the driver of this car. I had been in the car with John Jordan before on several journeys. I had picked up the vibe of his past. Something dark and damaging. They say the past informs the present. Well, this man's present seemed to be overwhelmed at times by the past. It hung out there just off the edges of each page.

Now, with this novel, Michael Lister brings the past across the margins and onto the page. Now you get to know things. Now you get to understand. It's a bold move by an author. The man with a mysterious past is a tried and true literary archetype. It worked with John Jordan for many years. Why mess with a good thing? Well, maybe because as a creator Lister wants to push things in from the margins and examine them and not rely on familiar archetypes. It's risky but the pay off can be high. It is here in *Innocent Blood.* Lister gives a unique edition to the John Jordan story. Another great ride with a very assured driver behind the wheel.

—Michael Connelly

Chapter One

In 1980 I came face to face with the Atlanta Child Murderer.

I was twelve years old. The same age as many of his victims.

This singular experience not only forever changed me, but actually altered the course of my life.

But long before this seminal visit to the city of Atlanta as a child, long before this encounter with evil, I was obsessed with the monster who was littering the woods of the metro area with the broken bodies of little black boys.

It had begun on July 21, 1979, when Edward Hope Smith went missing.

He was last seen leaving the Greenbriar Skating Rink on Stone Street, parting ways with his girlfriend at the intersection.

His body was discovered seven days later in a wooded area in a ravine just off Niskey Lake Road by a woman looking for cans. He had been shot with a .22 in the upper back. The area, surrounded by loblolly pines, white oaks, an occasional dogwood, and creeping kudzu vines, was a popular spot for people to dump their trash.

It was said that by the time his body was discovered, a vine from a nearby tree had already wrapped itself around the boy's lifeless neck.

My obsession had continued through the disappearance

and death of Timothy Hill, a thirteen-year-old boy and friend of an earlier victim, Jo-Jo Bell. Timothy went missing on March 13, 1981, and was last seen in the area of Lawson Street and Sells Avenue. His body was found seventeen days later on March 30th—the same day Ronald Reagan was shot by John Hinckley, Jr.—by a boater in the Chattahoochee River near Cochran Road. His partially submerged body was some twenty-five feet from the bank. The cause of death was determined to be asphyxia by suffocation.

There were other victims, of course, but they weren't children and I wasn't nearly as obsessed with them.

Children disappearing, dying, being discarded—some seventeen so far—held my developing mind hostage, seized my attention, captured my preteen imagination like nothing before ever had. And it was only partially because of the cruel and capricious nature of the killings, the fragility and vulnerability of childhood, and the fact that my dad, the sheriff of the small Florida Panhandle town were we lived, had a friend on the task force that was so ineffectually working the case. It was mostly because of how each and every little boy looked like and reminded me of my best friend in all the world, Merrill Monroe.

My fateful confrontation with the killer took place during the final weekend in November 1980, surrounded by gaudy gold Christmas decorations and to the soundtrack of traditional Christmas carols played through cheap speakers, the thin, electronic noises of video games, the wooden pop of pinball machines, and the desultory sounds of the city Sherman had burned to the ground.

Our parents had brought us to Atlanta, on what would be our final family vacation, to stay in the Omni hotel, to ice skate and shop, to play in the arcade and ride the gigantic escalator to the carnival in the clouds, to experience the spectacle of a hotel that could hold more people than lived in our entire little town.

While Nancy, Jake, and I skated and played, Mom drank and Christmas shopped, and Dad watched TV in the room when he wasn't meeting with his friend on the task force.

The Omni fit its name—all or of all things—for the mammoth structure seemed to my twelve-year-old self to contain all things. Whether shooting up several stories in seconds in the elevator or riding the enormous escalator to the fair or looking out the window of our room at the tiny figures ice skating below, the hotel held so very many larger-than-life and unexpected attractions, and yet retained an open and airy quality of hushed tones and lost sounds into which it seemed everything else in the world could easily fit.

Outside the hotel, fear and palpable racial tensions pulsed through the city. Inside, everyone whose job it was to cater to our comfort tried to pretend there *was* no world outside this one, but an uneasy anxiety coiled beneath the surface betrayed them—not unlike the one I sensed just behind the strained civility displayed by my parents.

It was during the afternoon of our second day that I saw him, the monster dressed like a man. And not just any man, a soft, slightly effeminate, light-skinned black man in a long-sleeved, large-collared silk shirt with thick wire-framed glasses and a big afro—only part of which was visible beneath a Braves baseball cap.

Nancy was teaching Jake to ice skate in the large round rink right in the center of the hotel. I was in the video game arcade trying to beat my best score on Space Invaders.

I had just failed to prevent the invasion when he walked in carrying a handful of flyers.

Unhurriedly and unapologetically he scoped out the arcade.

After identifying his marks, he began approaching black kids by themselves, handing each one a flyer, asking them if they wanted to be a star.

The flyers read: CAN YOU?? Sing or Play an Instrument

* If YOU Are Between "11-21" (male or female) And Would Like to Become A Professional Entertainer, "YOU" Can Apply for POSITIONS with Professional Recording Acts No experience is Necessary, Training is Provided. All Interviews Private & FREE!! *

There was something off about the man, some seeming contradiction between his arrogance and neediness, something loose and lascivious in the way he moved and looked at the kids around the arcade.

When he approached a short, scrawny kid of about ten years old in a blue turtleneck playing a KISS pinball machine, the kid shook his head without looking at him.

"Look at me, little brother," he said.

Continuing to play the game with intense concentration, he shook his head again without taking his eyes off the ball.

The creepy man then laid the flyer on the glass top of the pinball machine, blocking the boy's view and causing him to lose the turn.

"You heard of the Jackson Five, ain't ya? You could be like little Michael."

That stood out to me because I had just seen Michael Jackson in a silver-and-black sequined suit, backlit by a shimmering green light, performing "Rock with You" in the room before I came down, and he wasn't little anymore.

The boy abandoned his game and walked away with his head down.

When the dull-eyed, doughy young man followed, I stepped away from Space Invaders and in front of him.

"He said he's not interested," I said.

"Whoa, little man," he said, holding the hand without the flyers up in a placating gesture. "I'm just trying to help the youth of our city reach their potential."

I didn't say anything, just stood there.

On the same day all this happened, little LaMarcus Williams was murdered less than fifteen miles away from where we were standing at that moment. It would happen just six hours later in a place that would come to hold great significance for me, but it would be a full six years before I knew anything about it—when it became the first murder investigation I ever conducted.

"What's your name, boy?" he asked.

He had been leaning back considering me, eyeing me up and down, a bemused expression on his wrinkled black face.

I didn't respond, just held his gaze.

"Where you from?" he asked. "Ain't here, is it?"

Anger flashed in his face when I still refused to respond.

"Just 'cause I prefer chocolate don't mean I couldn't go for some vanilla," he said.

I still didn't respond, just stood there, every muscle in my undeveloped body tense. I wanted to look around, to see if there were any adults close by who might help, but I didn't want to break eye contact with him.

"I can make you talk little man," he said. "Make you do other things too."

My pounding heart was pumping adrenaline through me and I could feel myself beginning to shake.

He stepped toward me.

Just before I took a step back, there was a flash of movement behind me.

"What's going on here?" a security guard asked.

He had just come up behind us, a pale, thin, older white man in a too-big hotel security uniform.

"Nothin'. I's just leavin'. Little man here misunderstood my intentions. That's all. It's cool."

With that he turned and slowly swaggered away, down the game aisle and out the door.

If I had known then what I found out later—that the latest victim, Patrick "Pat Man" Rogers, had told Mary Harper that a man wanted to record his songs right before he went missing, I might have been even more suspicious, might have said something to someone about the soft man with the handful of flyers harassing kids in the arcade of the Omni hotel, and I might have actually saved the several victims still to come.

But I didn't know and I didn't act and it has haunted me ever since the moment when—seven months later, on June 21, 1981—Wayne Williams was arrested, and the satan who had laid siege to South Atlanta and frightened a nation finally had an all too human face.

Chapter Two

During the seven months leading up to the arrest, unaware I had actually met the man the manhunt was for, I feverishly followed every step of the investigation—all the media coverage, every report of a missing child, every discovery of another dead body.

Dad fed me what information his friend on the task force was feeding him, and I ate it like a crazed starved thing.

All through the Christmas season, I observed and obsessed, studied and stewed, but no children disappeared and no other bodies were discovered in December.

The holiday break ended and I returned to school.

Then Lubie Geter went missing on January 3rd.

He was last seen at the Stewart-Lakewood Shopping Center selling Zep Gel car deodorizers outside the Big Star Food Store. He was wearing a purple coat, a green shirt, blue jeans, and brown loafers.

From the moment I heard he was missing until his body was discovered on February 5th, I vividly imagined the horrors he was subjected to and then pictured his lifeless brown body decaying in the woods of Decatur every time I closed my eyes.

While Geter's family and the nation waited for news of his fate, a friend of his, Terry Pue, disappeared on January 22nd. When I heard this I lost even the tiny broken fragment of hope

I had that Lubie might still be alive.

Terry Pue was last seen spending the night in a fast food restaurant on Memorial Drive and trading bottles for money at a nearby shopping center.

The next day, his body was found off Sigman Road in Rockdale County. He had abrasions on his elbows and bruises on his head and died of asphyxiation by ligature strangulation.

On February 5th, Lubie Geter's body was found by a dog off Vandiver Road. He was wearing only his white jockey shorts. His Levi's blue jeans and brown belt were found a short distance away inside a brown paper bag three feet deep in a creek. He died of asphyxiation by manual strangulation and his body had been mutilated by animals.

During this time, I was living an uneventful small-town life. School. Basketball. Birthday parties. Sleepovers. Chores. TV. All the while preoccupied by Atlanta, the slaughter of the susceptible, the woeful wails of the inconsolable, the citywide search for a seemingly supernatural serial killer.

Mom and Dad argued about how much he should share with me about the case. Mom and Dad argued about everything.

The world kept spinning and Atlanta's children kept disappearing. And dying. Two in February. Two more in March.

So much death. So much decay. So much despair.

And then it stopped. Or seemed to.

On May 22nd at three o'clock in the morning, Wayne Williams was pulled over by an Atlanta police patrol car and a second unmarked car with federal agents in it. His 1970 Chevrolet station wagon had been spotted turning around and driving back across the James Jackson Parkway/South Cobb Drive bridge immediately following an officer staked-out beneath the bridge hearing a loud splash in the water of the Chattahoochee River.

Later that same day, Williams was questioned by FBI agents at his parents' home where he lived.

Two days later, on May 24th, the naked body of Nathaniel Cater was found floating downriver just a few miles from the bridge.

On June 3rd, Wayne Williams was questioned again by FBI agents at their headquarters about discrepancies in his statements. He was also administered a polygraph examination that showed he was being deceptive. Later that same day, his home and vehicle were searched.

On June 4th, Williams called a press conference, addressing what was happening and answering questions from the media.

When I saw him on TV, I told my family about what had happened in the Omni arcade back in November.

"Are you sure?" Mom had asked.

Dad nodded his certainty and support. "You realize," he said, "you may have very well saved that little boy's life—him or another kid he could've picked up there that day."

I hadn't thought of that.

"Do I need to give a statement?" I asked Dad.

"I don't want him involved," Mom said.

"*I'm already involved.*"

"I doubt it'll be necessary," Dad said, "but I'll call Frank and ask him."

Late that night I found my dad dozing in front of the TV and gave him a handwritten statement I had worked all evening on.

"I'll get it to the task force," he said.

I nodded and turned to walk out of the room.

"Proud of you," he said, squinting at the sheet of notebook paper I had just given him.

On June 21st, Wayne Williams was arrested.

That evening I was reading in my room when Nancy's best friend and my secret crush, Anna, had come in.

"Hey," she said.

"Hey."

I dropped the book onto the nightstand and sat up, making room for her on the bed beside me.

I had fallen in love with Anna when she wasn't looking.

She hadn't been looking, but I had. I had watched her closely, studied her carefully, seen what no one else had, what no one else could have.

As her best friend's younger brother I had been in the utterly unique position to see her soul.

I said I had fallen in love with Anna but that's not right.

I hadn't fallen in love with her at all. I had grown to love her. Or rather love had grown in me for her, while observing her during a million different unguarded moments—moments in which her kindness and goodness, her fierceness and ferocity, her wit and wisdom, had been made manifest.

"Nancy told me what happened to you in Atlanta," she said. "I'm so glad nothing bad happened to you."

"Thanks."

She was wearing the green ribbon I had given her. It was a sign of solidarity with the children of Atlanta. People all across the nation were wearing them—including Robert De Niro when he had won his Best Actor Oscar for *Raging Bull* a few months back—but we were the only two people in Pottersville wearing them and it meant more to me than she would ever know.

"How're you feeling?"

I shrugged.

The truth was I was feeling everything—excited, relieved, scared, confused, disappointed, unsatisfied.

"I still can't believe you saw him," she said. "Stood up to him. Looked him in the face and . . . your dad's right. You saved someone's life."

I didn't know what to say so I didn't say anything, just looked at how beautiful she was.

"I'm just so relieved," she said. "So glad you didn't get hurt. But I'm also so proud of you. Standing up to him like that.

You're . . . just . . . so . . . Do you mind if I hug you?"

I didn't. Just the opposite, in fact, but she didn't wait to hear it from me.

Suddenly, I was being hugged by the girl I most wanted to be hugged by in all the world.

I could feel the heat emanating from my skin.

She held me for a long time, her developed body pressing into mine, our cheeks touching, her hair falling onto my face.

She smelled and felt even better than all my imagining told me she would.

In a little while, when she had let go of me and life wasn't as rich, as sweet, as good as it had been a few moments before, she said, "It's hard to believe he killed nearly thirty people."

"He didn't," I said with the conviction and certainty of a child. "He didn't even kill most of 'em."

"Really?"

"Really," I said. "It'll be a while before we know. Hell, we may never know, but I'll bet you a . . . another hug . . . that he did as few as ten and at most maybe thirteen or fourteen."

"You don't have to wait that long for another hug," she said. "And you don't have to bet me for it. I'll give you another anytime you like."

"Then how about a kiss," I said.

She smiled and blushed a little herself.

"It's a bet," she said. "Now let's hug on it."

We hugged again.

"I'm so glad you're in the world, John Jordan. The world needs you. So glad."

I hugged her harder.

She had no idea of the effect of those words on me or how for the rest of my life they would ring in my ears as I recalled this moment over and over and over again.

"Wait," she said, pulling back. "Who killed all those

other people?"

"I have no idea," I said, "but I intend to find out."

Chapter Three

In one of the greatest ironies in criminal history, the Atlanta Child Murderer wasn't arrested, charged with, or tried for killing a single child.

Wayne Williams was indicted and tried for killing Nathaniel Cater, the twenty-seven-year-old victim pulled from the river two days after Williams had been stopped near the James Jackson bridge, and Jimmy Ray Payne, a twenty-one-year-old young man who went missing on April 22nd after leaving home en route to the Omni. He was found five days later on April 27th, his body pulled from the Chattahoochee River two hundred yards south of the I-285 bridge.

No one—not Wayne Williams, not anyone—was ever charged with the murder of any children.

Not a single one.

This bothered me more than anything else, except the fact that they were killed in the first place.

My frustration and obsession and anger and confusion continued, intensified.

So much was happening, both in my small world and in the wide world beyond it—I became a teenager, my parents split up and eventually divorced, Anna got a boyfriend and broke my heart, Mom's drinking increased, I had a spiritual awakening, Bob Marley died, the CDC reported five cases of homosexual men with weakened immune systems, Charles and Diana had a wedding in front of the whole world—but all of it, everything happening everywhere, dimmed a bit, receded into the background, overwhelmed by the foreground light of the case against Williams and the trial intending to bring him to some sort of justice.

Jury selection started on December 8, 1981. After six days, the twelve people—eight black and four white—selected and charged with delivering a verdict consisted of nine women and three men.

"He's not even being tried for a single child's death," I said to Dad.

I had just come in from basketball practice and found him watching the news coverage of the case.

I was sore from the brawl-like scrimmage I had just participated in. I was raw-bone weary from not sleeping and the mental, emotional, and psychological fatigue that resulted from obsessing over Wayne Williams and what was happening in Atlanta.

"I know, but—"

"It's not right."

I was supposed to be at home by now. Mom was expecting me for dinner, but my new routine was to have Coach drop me at Dad's after practice to talk to him about the case before walking the mile or so to Mom's.

When the coverage concluded, Dad asked me to step over to the TV and turn down the sound.

I did.

Dad's new bachelor pad had very little furniture, but he did have a brand new big television hooked up to cable, which had only recently arrived in Pottersville.

"Some of them will be admitted as evidence," he said.

"Whatta you mean?"

"Prosecutor will introduce them as pattern cases to show

Williams had a pattern."

In fact, ten pattern cases were ultimately used—more than any other case before or since.

"But if they're part of the pattern and are going to be used, why not charge him with them too?"

"It's a strategy," he said. "That's all. Frank says the prosecutor's trial plan is built around what happened on the James Jackson Bridge on May 22nd because he can actually place Williams at the scene. And he's got an eyewitness who says he saw Williams holding hands with Cater earlier that night. He's using Jimmy Ray Payne because he can tie him to the same location. If he overcharges and brings in all the others, he runs the risk of them being insufficient in law to sustain a conviction. By doing it this way he can still use some of the others to prove identity, bent of mind, knowledge, intent, course of contact—things like that. He wants to get a conviction the surest way possible. And he doesn't want to overwhelm or confuse the jury. Williams only has one life to serve."

I shook my head.

His phone rang.

"That'll be your mom looking for you," he said. "Better get goin'. Need to get out of those wet clothes anyway. I'm sure she's got supper ready."

"Yes, sir."

"How're things at home?"

I shrugged.

"She drinkin'?" he asked.

"She breathin'?" I said.

"*Hey*," he said. "I know it's . . . I know it's not easy sometimes . . . but always show respect to your mother."

"Yes, sir."

"And as far as Williams goes . . . He's guilty and they're gonna get him. Don't forget that's what matters most."

"But—"

"Remember, there are no fingerprints, no eyewitnesses

who ever saw Williams hurt or kill anyone. It's a circumstantial case."

The case primarily rested on transfer or trace evidence—carpet fibers and dog hairs found on the victims, hairs and fibers allegedly from Williams's environment, his home and car—proving contact between the victims and Williams.

"It's a thin case," I said. "They've got Williams on the bridge. They've got fibers and dog hairs. What else have they got?"

"You don't think he's the killer?"

"I think it's a thin case," I said. "And yeah, I think he's a killer. I even think he killed a few of the ones he's supposed to have."

Chapter Four

The trial began on January 6, 1982.

It was presided over by Clarence Cooper, the first black judge elected to the Fulton County bench and a former assistant district attorney. The most active member of the prosecutorial team was Jack Mallard, whose nickname was Blood because of the way he went for the jugular. The defense attorney was Mary Welcome, a popular black lawyer and a former Atlanta city solicitor.

For the prosecution it was a splash in the river beneath a bridge, a suspicious station wagon above, a young man out at three in the morning with a dubious story, eyewitnesses connecting that young man with the victims, a pudgy, bespectacled, frustrated homosexual Jekyll and Hyde, carpet fibers and dog hairs, ten uncharged pattern cases.

For the defense it was the wrong man—a good, gentle, soft, weak, harmless guy—refuting witnesses, calling into question evidence, an upstate New York hospital pathologist specializing in pediatrics contradicting autopsy results, a weather service hydrologist claiming Cater's body would not have ended up where it did had it been dropped from the James Jackson Parkway Bridge, and of course, Wayne Bertram Williams himself, confidently spouting protestations, proclaiming his innocence—a witness for the defense who may have done far more for the prosecution.

The pattern cases became the key factor for evidence to be used by the state against Williams, especially when linking similar fibers. By themselves the Cater and Payne cases were extremely weak, but by introducing evidence from each of the ten pattern cases, the prosecution was able to enter eyewitnesses and fiber connections among many of the victims.

The ten pattern cases used were Alfred Evans, Eric Middlebrooks, Charles Stephens, William Barrett, Terry Pue, John Porter, Lubie Geter, Joseph Bell, Patrick Baltazar, and Larry Rogers.

The characteristics of the pattern cases were that the victims were black males, street hustlers, from poor families, no evidence of forced abduction, from broken homes, no apparent motives for their disappearances, killed by asphyxiation by strangulation. None of them owned a car, their bodies were found near expressway ramps or major arteries and transported before or after death, they were all missing clothing when found, and they all had similar fibers found on them.

The prosecution called a successful black businessman, Eustis Blakely, and his wife because they were friends with Williams. They were asked if they knew Williams to lie and exaggerate. Blakely testified Williams had told him that he flew fighter jets at Dobbins Air Force base—something Blakely knew to be a lie because of how bad Williams's eyesight was.

Far more incriminating was the testimony of Blakely's wife. She had asked Williams after he had become a suspect if the police got enough evidence on him would he confess before he got hurt. He told her he would. She also testified that Williams told her he could knock out black street kids in a few minutes by putting his hands on their necks.

When cross-examined, the defense attorney asked if she was implying Williams had killed someone. She answered that she was, that she was sorry but she really did believe that he had.

Lugene Laster testified that he saw Jo-Jo Bell get into a Chevrolet station wagon driven by a man he identified as Williams. Robert Henry, who knew Cater, testified he saw Cater and Williams holding hands the evening of the bridge incident. A couple of youths claimed Williams made sexual advances toward them and a fifteen-year-old said Williams paid him two dollars to let him fondle his genitals.

Two other witnesses, a nightclub owner and a recreational director, discredited Williams's statements that earlier in the evening on the night of the May 22nd bridge incident he was picking up a tape recorder and playing basketball.

The defense put a number of witnesses on the stand to rebut what prosecution witnesses had said about Williams's behavior or where he was at a particular time. They even had a college student who had been recruited by Williams for a singing job testify that Williams disliked homosexuals and expected his clients to have high standards and morals, and a woman who claimed to having had what she called normal sex with Williams.

To refute time of death in the Nathaniel Cater case, the defense brought in its own expert who lost credibility when he testified that Cater had been in the water for at least two weeks—far less time than he had even been missing.

Others were called. No one was particularly helpful or even effective.

Finally, Williams himself took the stand.

He challenged eyewitness accounts and made it clear to the jury he was too small and weak to have quickly stopped the car on the bridge and thrown Cater over the shoulder-high guard rail into the river.

He also continually attempted to convince the jury he didn't possess the temperament to commit murder. Something he seemed more or less successful at doing until cross.

Under a lengthy, skillful, aggressive cross examination Williams snapped.

Wayne Williams was no match for Jack Mallard.

Mallard would lull Williams with lengthy, repetitive questions about seemingly small details or fine points, and then pounce. One of his associates described it as slowly pulling the hammer back and eventually letting it fall.

On the third day of cross, Mallard let the hammer drop.

As if Williams was an inadequate sparring partner, Mallard jabbed and moved, peppering him with punches, setting him up for the knockout.

Mallard used Williams's own contradictions against him and confronted him with all the lies and exaggerations and testimony and evidence and illogical and inane statements and claims he had made.

And Williams came undone.

"You want the real Wayne Williams?" he asked. "You got him right here."

Williams transformed into something the jury had heretofore not seen.

Jekyll became Hyde. The Gemini was unleashed and the defendant became a witness for the prosecution.

On Saturday, February 27, 1982, at about seven in the evening, after only eleven hours of deliberation, the jury returned its verdict.

Wayne Bertram Williams was found guilty on both counts of murder and immediately sentenced to two life sentences.

But it was ultimately unsatisfying.

I was left with far more questions than answers.

Which of the victims had Williams actually killed?

Who had killed the others?

Would anyone ever stand trial for killing the kids?

The end of the trial was just the beginning of the investigation for me.

I spent the rest of my time in high school studying the case and preparing to become a cop.

While the world was being introduced to MTV and AIDS and the personal computer, while Michael Jackson was making and releasing the biggest-selling album of all time, while Challenger was falling from the sky, I was working on the Wayne Williams case and, with my dad's help, on a fast track to becoming a certified law enforcement officer.

Chapter Five

"You okay?" Merrill asked.

I didn't respond. I couldn't think of an answer that wasn't a lie.

He had found me in the bottom of an abandoned boat at the landing, sleeping it off, still clutching Mom's stolen vodka to me like a baby with a bottle.

I sat up slowly, the spinning world around me streaking by in blurs of blue and green, brown and burnt-orange, and surveyed the dusky evening.

"Thinkin' about takin' a boat ride?" he said.

"Came out here to swim," I said, holding up the bottle.

"That's not swimming. It's drowning."

I nodded. He was right and I knew it. I just didn't know what to do about it.

He was big even back then, but, like the rest of us, still hadn't fully grown into his features. Teeth and ears still slightly too big. He was wearing his basketball warmups over his uniform, the cheap fabric straining over the roping cable cords of his muscles.

"Missed you at the game today," he said. "Coulda used that jumper of yours. Lost by five."

"Not playin' anymore," I said.

"Call it what it is," he said. "Not playing anymore sound

better than quitting."

"I'm quitting. Don't have the time."

"'Cause of takin' up swimmin'?"

"Yeah."

"Well, let's go tell Coach. He needs to know his best shooter sidelinin' hisself."

"I'm sure he's figured it out."

"Nah, I just left him at the gym. He perplexed as the rest of us."

"I'll tell him tomorrow at school," I said.

"Oh, you comin' to school tomorrow?"

"Believe I will."

He didn't say anything and we were both silent as the last of the sun streaking the treetops to the west finally faded out and the light in the landing changed.

After a while he said, "Tell me how I can help you."

"Would if I could," I said.

"I've been doing this a while," Dad said.

"What?"

"Law enforcement. Investigating. And I've picked up a thing or two."

I didn't say anything, just listened.

It was 1985, my junior year of high school.

It was report card day and my grades had continued their recent trend of declining, which, I assumed, was why he was in my room.

I had stopped all extracurricular activities. I had pulled back to one degree or another from any and everything but my own personal investigation into the Atlanta Child Murders.

Maps of Atlanta hung on my walls next to bad copies of crime scene, suspect, and victim photos. Stacks of witness statements, evidence reports, UNSUB profiles, and lab documents were scattered about. The small space looked far more like a squad room than a seventeen-year-old boy's bedroom.

"You're gonna drive yourself crazy if you're not careful. You've got a gift. You do. I can see it. It's rare. You're gonna make a great investigator—but only if you don't burn yourself out first."

He didn't often compliment me or anyone else. Hell, he seldom spoke. This gave all his words weight—and his compliments the impact of a punch.

"A case like this . . . " he said.

He trailed off and what for me at the time was *the* case hung there between us.

"It's . . . got . . . its own . . . I don't know . . . darkness, its own power. Maybe even presence. It's evil like you'll rarely encounter. A black hole you can lose yourself in."

I had never heard him talk like this but I knew exactly what he meant and knew why he was pressing himself outside his normal, familiar, comfortable space to do it.

"I'm worried about you," he said. "And it's not the grades. They're a symptom. Everything's a symptom. The isolation. The drinking. The sleeplessness. Symptoms of the obsession, of the frustration, of . . . how . . . close you are . . . to the void."

I nodded. Not because I agreed with his assessment but because I understood what he was saying and appreciated his concern.

I didn't know anyone except maybe Merrill knew I was drinking and not sleeping. And I knew for sure he hadn't said anything to anyone. Everything about this conversation told me my dad was a far better cop and man than my self-involved teenage self knew.

"The thing about it, son," he said, his voice gentle, entreating, "is the empathy you feel with the victims, the unquenchable thirst burning inside you for justice . . . for restoring some kind of order . . . the rage you feel at the murderer . . . the obsession with knowing, with uncovering, with finding the truth . . . They are the very things that make you perfect for this kind of work . . . but also a perfect candidate for this kind of work to crush, to chew up, and . . . and I think I can see it already starting to."

"I'm okay," I said.

"I don't think you are," he said, looking around at the glut of investigative documents and photographs that cluttered the room. "And I'm the reason you have most of this. I've encouraged you but I haven't really guided you, taught you, helped you."

"You've helped me a lot."

"Help you find a balance," he said. "Help you with how to let go."

"*Let go?*"

"The case is over, son," he said. "Williams is serving two life sentences. The murders stopped. Why can't you move on? What else is there to—"

"The murders didn't stop," I said.

"What?"

"Here," I said. "Sit down."

I swept off a pile of papers on my desk chair and he sat down.

"A lot of people believe Wayne Williams is innocent," I said, "but nobody with any credibility believes he killed all twenty-eight or -nine who made the task force list. There were two girls. There were adults, not just young black teens. Some of the victims were stabbed. Some were shot. Some asphyxiated with a ligature, others with bare hands. If Wayne Williams is the Atlanta Child Murderer and he strangled the young boys, why wasn't he tried for that? And why wasn't anyone charged with any of the other murders? If it wasn't him, an innocent man is going to die in prison for something someone else did, and the real killer remains free. Can you live with that?"

He seemed to think about it for a moment, but as it

turned out he was thinking of something else entirely.

"Son, there's someone I want you to talk to, and your mom and I think it's best if you come live with me for a while."

Chapter Six

When Dad had said he wanted me to talk to someone, I had assumed he meant a shrink, so I was as surprised as I was relieved when I found out it was a cop.

The cop, an L.A. detective with the same name as an Early Netherlandish painter whose work I had encountered in an art appreciation class earlier in the year, had impressed Dad during some special training on serial sex crime investigation he had attended in L.A.

The training had followed Ted Bundy's rampage in Tallahassee at FSU's Chi Omega sorority house. Something about the viciousness of the attacks, their relative proximity to Pottersville, and the fact that the victims had been the same age as my older sister Nancy, really affected Dad, and for a while it seemed all he did was travel for training.

"Y'all share the same relentlessness and obsession," Dad had said. "He's found a way to make it work. He's one of if not *the* best cop you'll ever encounter. Listen to what he has to say. He won't say much, but what he does will help you."

Words of praise like those from Jack Jordan were beyond rare. They were the only ones like them I ever heard him utter. For him to say I shared any traits at all with such a detective did more for me than anything save the conversation itself.

The conversation took place on my second night living with him.

Not only had Dad taken the trouble to set it up, but he was letting me stay up late to take the West Coast call.

I was alone in the quiet, mostly empty house when the call came.

Dispatch had requested that Dad return to his office to deal with a disturbance in the jail just minutes before—something that actually made me far less self-conscious about having the conversation.

The TV was off and the only sound I could hear in the small, carpeted house was that of my own reflexive respiration. The ringing phone shattered the silence, and like so many serendipitous occurrences during this significant and seminal time for me, the call changed my life.

"John?"

"Yes, sir."

"It's Harry Bosch. No need to call me sir."

I felt an instant affinity with the detective who treated me like an adult, and the disembodied voice from the opposite side of the continent suddenly seemed far more like a brother than a stranger.

"Thank you for taking the time to call," I said. "I hear you're working a pretty big case right now."

"No problem," he said. "Sorry it couldn't be any earlier."

Faintly, in the background, beneath the voice and the static and white noise, I could hear the soft, soothing sounds of a lone alto saxophone.

There was something kind of sad and lonely about the sax that made me feel neither sad nor lonely, as if someone else feeling such things and expressing them in such ways helped abate them somehow.

I was unsure what to say next so I waited.

When he didn't say anything either, there was a moment of awkwardness—at least for me.

The silence set an early tone for what would be a conversation with a lot of quiet in it, and I could tell that Harry Bosch, like so many of the men I admired and attempted to emulate, was restrained and self-contained.

"Jack tells me you're gonna be a cop," he said eventually. "Says you've got all the makings of a great one."

"That's not what he tells me," I said.

He didn't respond right away and I wondered if what I said had sounded disrespectful.

"I just meant . . . he's worried about me. It's why he asked you to call. I think he thinks I'm too . . . I don't know. Like obsessed or . . . something."

"Whatta you think?"

I couldn't believe he was asking me.

I thought about it for a moment.

"Not sure. Maybe. I just don't know. Maybe I am. I . . . I don't know any other way to be. I really don't. He keeps tellin' me I've got to let it go, got to be more . . . balanced or something, but I can't—not when kids have been killed, not when those who should be tryin' to solve their murders aren't, not when nobody else seems to care anymore."

I paused for a moment but continued when all I heard was the hum of the line.

"All those kids matter," I said. "All of them. They all count—not just white kids, not just rich kids, not just victims from cases that are easy to solve or that have a perp who can be prosecuted."

"Don't ever forget that," he said. "Everybody counts."

"No, sir, I won't."

Here was someone who understood, who got it.

More quiet followed. More static on the line reaching across the more than two thousand miles between us. And more music.

Harry getting it made me feel the way the music did. Less alone in the world somehow.

"Listen, John, I'm not big on handing out advice . . . I'm

no expert . . . but the work matters. The victims matter. When they don't, I'd say it's time to stop."

Exactly, I thought. That's exactly it.

"The thing is . . ."

Here it comes, I thought. Here's where he agrees with Dad and undermines everything he's said so far.

"You've got to be able to do the work," he said.

That was not what I was expecting.

I thought about it.

He was right. I couldn't say the work really mattered to me if I wasn't going to do what it took to be able to keep doing it. Caring about victims, wanting everybody to count, being relentless, it wasn't enough. I had to be able to keep doing it.

The jazz saxophone stopped momentarily then started again.

"I'm not sure what else I can tell you," he said. "I'm still trying to figure it out myself."

It seemed like that was all he had to say, but he didn't end the conversation or the call, just waited.

He didn't seem to be in a hurry to hang up, and I wanted to extend the exchange if I could.

"Can I ask you . . . how you deal with the darkness?" I said.

"Probably have to ask someone else about that," he said.

I appreciated that he didn't feel the need that most adults did to have an answer for everything, but I wondered if the question bothered him.

Dad had told me he had been a tunnel rat in Vietnam so I knew he knew all about the dark. Of course that didn't mean he knew what to do about it or what to tell me to do about it.

"It's a good question. Keep asking it. I think it's different for everyone. Figuring out what works for you is part of the process. That make sense?"

I nodded before I realized he couldn't see me doing it.

"Yes, sir," I said. "It really does."

"Figure out a way to function," he said. "Not sure it has to be any harder than that."

I thought about it for a long moment, during which all he did was wait.

Something Nietzsche said about monsters shimmered at the edges of my memory. What was it? Beware of catching monsters, or something similar.

"Wish I could help you more," he said.

"You've helped me far more than you'll ever know."

"You need me," he said, "you call me. And don't take too much shit from Jack, okay?"

After we hung up, I sat there and thought about all the wisdom that one conversation contained, replaying it over and over in my head.

Before I went to bed, I looked up the Nietzsche quote. *Beware that, when fighting monsters, you yourself do not become a monster.*

In my dream it became part of my conversation with Harry Bosch—a conversation that took place not over a telephone but over an autopsy table holding the body of Patrick "Pat Man" Rogers, in an old-fashioned operating theater in Atlanta with Wayne Williams watching from the gallery above us.

Chapter Seven

How can I describe what happened next?

Simply this. Something.

Something unexpected. Something inexplicable and ineffable.

Something undeniable.

Someone flipped a switch somewhere inside me. And then what exactly?—light, warmth, insight, enlightenment? Some formerly fallow ground began to burst forth with new life. Seed, water, nourishment, and a small shoot broke the surface of the soil. I woke up. Shaken from my slumber I came to consciousness.

It was not unlike falling in love.

It happened during my senior year of high school, this transformation, this moment of clarity, this line in the sand of my life, which would forever be the demarcation between before and after for me.

One day I was one way. The next another.

One moment I was walking in one direction. The next moment another.

It was extraordinary.

It changed everything.

Merrill's mom recognized it first.

Our eyes met and she saw and she smiled.

"Well now, look at the new you," she said.

I had just walked into the tiny kitchen of her small clapboard house where she was hard at work on the best fried chicken, collard greens, and cornbread anyone ever made. Ever.

She immediately stopped cooking, turned off the old gas oven, and took a seat at the narrow, wobbly, Formica top kitchen table.

"Dinner can wait," she said. "Sit down and tell Mama Monroe all about it."

Merrill had yet to come in from baseball practice. We were alone in the cramped, creaky house, the best and safest place I had yet found on the planet.

I sat down.

"Not sure I can say," I said.

"That's good," she said. "Real good."

I must have looked confused.

"Be little that had happened, you could 'splain it, baby."

I looked at her and smiled.

"That the only bit of Shakespeare Mama knows. 'Course I changed it up a little, but . . . it always stuck with me."

As usual, she had a dip of Honey Bee Sweet Snuff that poked out the skin beneath her bottom lip a bit and caused her to contort her mouth some as she spoke.

"What did?"

"'I were but little happy if I could say how much,'" she said.

"So true," I said. "Were but little changed if I could say how much. That's exactly it. Exactly right."

"Paul got knocked on his ass on the road to Damascus," she said. "Never knew what hit him. Jesus went down in the water one way, came up another. Moses came up on a burnin' bush that didn't burn up."

I nodded. "I read that when they asked Siddhartha what happened to him, he just said he woke up."

"Who?"

"The Buddha."

"Mama don't know nothin' 'bout no Buddha, baby, but she do know when the Holy Ghost done come on one of her boys."

I smiled, happy to be one of her boys.

Reaching behind her, she removed her spit cup from the counter beside the stove, spit in it, then placed it on the table in front of her. Inside the faded plastic FSU stadium cup was a couple of folded paper towels to help soak up the powered snuff and spit.

"You been touched by the hand of God," she said, wiping her mouth. "His shekinah glory is all over you, boy. Shines on your face, through your eyes. You'll never be the same again."

I wouldn't use the language she was, but I knew what she meant—and she was right about the last at least. I would never be the same again.

"I've been worried about you," she said. "Prayin' for you. Prayin' Lord Jesus help my JJ find his way."

"I've been in a bad way," I said.

She nodded. "Obsessin' over those poor black children," she said.

I thought about the darkness that entered my head and heart through the Atlanta Child Murders case, how heavy I had been, how angry and frustrated, and how much I had been drinking lately.

"Among other things, yes, ma'am."

"Frettin', worryin', weight of the whole world on your bony little shoulders, boy."

I nodded.

"Listen to me, son," she said. "God give you a good mind. You some kinda smart and got such a good heart, but let me tell you somethin'—you think your mind's your friend but it ain't. Just remember that. My mind is not my friend. It's not my boss. It's not me. It's a spirited horse needs controllin'. Understand? Don't let your mind run wild. Don't let it make you a slave."

I thought about it.

"What happened to you, happened here," she said, tapping my chest with the back of her meaty, misshapen brown hand. "Not here," she added, placing her fingertips on my forehead and giving it a good push. "Don't forget it. God's in your guts. In your heart. Not your head."

"Yes, ma'am."

She didn't say anything, just waited, spitting into her cup again as she did.

When I didn't say anything either, she said, "Well?"

"I had taken a bottle of vodka to the landing," I said, "but when I got there, the evening sky was so radiant, so . . . I've never seen anything quite like it. Plum-colored background, streaked with brilliant fiery flamingo feathers of pink and orange, all of which was mirrored on the glass-like surface of the water below. And there was a quality to the light, a feel to the place, a presence, a . . . it was palpable . . . a . . . I don't know . . . like a . . . holy hush I guess. It was so beautiful, so peaceful. Nothing moved. Nothing at all. I poured out the bottle . . . almost like an offering or . . . And then a small wind whirled up, troubling the surface of the waters, causing leaves to dance toward me as it came on shore. As it surrounded me—it wasn't blowing anywhere else in the entire area but right around me—I . . . I heard a voice, whispering to me from the wind."

She nodded and smiled as I trailed off, reliving for the moment the magic I had been so moved by.

After a while, I'm not sure how long, she said, "What is it, son?"

"Ma'am?"

"Somethin' changed. Somethin's troublin' you, boy?"

"Everything's changed," I said. "I feel this . . . urge to . . . help people . . . to try to share and . . . I can't be a cop now, can't just move to Atlanta after high school and work the case like I planned, can't just . . . But . . . I can't let my dad down either. He's invested so much in my becoming a . . . to follow him in . . ."

"Follow your guts, boy," she said. "Who knows? Ol' Jack Jordan may surprise you . . . or . . . you might surprise yourself at what you can do. Don't limit God. Don't think you got to be a this or that, fit here not there, all or nothin'. You just trust and obey. Trust and obey. God will make a way."

Chapter Eight

"Jack tells me you think the task force got it wrong," Frank said.

Frank Morgan, a middle-aged, gray-haired, Georgia Bureau of Investigations agent and Dad's friend on the Atlanta Missing and Murdered Children task force, had come to Mexico Beach for vacation and we had driven down to see him.

He was a tall, trim man with wire-framed glasses that darkened in the sun, a good, straight-talking, straight-edged guy, rigid, humorless, nerdish.

It was in the late spring of '86 just a month or so before I would graduate from high school, and though I had had a spiritual awakening of sorts and found a modicum of equilibrium, I had not been able to completely let go of my obsessive connection to the case.

"I never said y'all got it wrong," I said.

"You think Williams is innocent?"

I shrugged.

"You're not one of those who says there's no such thing as black serial killers, are you?"

"No. I'm not. I know there are, know there have been far more than what most people realize."

"But you don't think Williams is one. You think he's innocent."

"No. Not necessarily. More not proven."

"Well, that'd be on the prosecution not the task force, but it was proven to the satisfaction of the jury who heard the entire case made and the defense against it."

He was defensive but not overly so.

We were on the front porch of his small, old rented cottage across the street from the beach, in early evening.

The sun was on its way to setting. Soon it would slip behind the sea at the vanishing point of the horizon. But for now it hung in the west just above and beyond the Gulf.

Frank was grilling hamburgers, he and Dad drinking beer from the bottle.

Frank's family, a wife and a preteen boy and girl, were at the water's edge, collecting sea shells and sticking their toes in the Gulf.

"So what's your beef with the task force?" Frank asked.

"It didn't finish its job."

"Only because the killer's in prison instead of the ground."

"Whose killer? The two adults? Cater and Payne? Those are the only ones he's serving time for."

"Do you know what would've happened if he had been tried for all the murders?" he said.

"He'd've walked," I said. "Because he didn't commit all the murders, but thanks to how everything was handled there's doubt to whether he committed any."

"Oh, trust me. He did. But you're right. He didn't do all of them."

"The list—" I began.

"That damn list," he said.

"So many different victims—not just young black boys, but girls, adults—different methods of murder."

He nodded. "You're right. Don't blame me for that damn list. I didn't create it. And I kept saying the list is shit.

There were victims that should've been on it that weren't and others that should've never been added in the first place."

"A serial killer has a pattern," I said. "He commits serial crimes—all part of a series that can be linked together. Serial killers have a signature. What's the pattern in this case? Which victims are part of the series? What is the killer's signature?"

"It's not that simple," he said. "Just wait 'til you work your first case, let alone a case like this. There are always things that don't make sense, that you can't answer, that will drive you crazy if you let them. Always. We're dealing with deranged human beings."

He paused and flipped the burgers with the large spatula he was holding.

"That being said," he continued, "there was a pattern. But instead of me telling you, you tell me. Let's hear what you think."

"Okay. The only pattern cases were those of the asphyxiated and dumped young black boys. That's the series."

He nodded. "Like the ones the prosecution used in the case—the pattern victims linked to Williams."

"So why was he tried for killing two adults?"

"Because they could tie him to the bridge."

"But if he killed Nathaniel Cater and threw his body off the bridge, doesn't that break the pattern? Wouldn't that mean Williams wasn't the killer of the boys?"

"You don't think killers kill outside of their pattern? Occasionally? Sometimes? Out of necessity if nothing else."

"Sure," I said. "I'm sure you're right, but doesn't it bother you that he was tried for the anomaly and not the pattern?"

"Everything about the whole goddamn thing bothers me," he said. "Everything."

"You don't think it's possible Williams isn't the killer?" I asked.

"If he's not, why'd the killings stop?"

"Did they?" I asked.

"You saying they didn't?"

"There have been other, similar killings in the area," I said. "But they could've stopped for a different reason."

"Which would be?"

"The killer moved, was killed, or incarcerated."

"It's possible," he said. "Highly, highly unlikely, but remotely possible."

"There's a man in prison right now who was a prime suspect in one of the pattern killings, who eyewitnesses say killed Clifford Jones."

"You mean Jamie Brooks?"

I nodded. "And he went to prison around the same time most of the murders stopped."

"Let's say Jamie Brooks did kill Clifford Jones," he said. "The witness was discredited, but let's say he did. He and Calvin Smith. That doesn't mean Williams didn't kill the others."

"No, *but* the green trilobal fiber that was supposed to tie Williams to the pattern cases was found on Clifford Jones. So if it was Jamie Brooks, suddenly he's tied to all the pattern cases."

Frank looked at Dad. "Smart kid," he said, pointing at me with the spatula. "Gonna make a great cop."

Dad sighed and shook his head. "He's decided to go a different direction."

"What?" Frank asked.

"What a waste, right?" Dad said. "Tell him. Now he wants to be a preacher instead."

Frank looked at me.

I shook my head.

"Not a preacher, no, but in ministry."

"Wants to save the world," Dad said.

"Not the world, no. Not save anybody . . . just . . . I . . . I just want . . . to help people."

"You've got a gift," Frank said. "And there are worse ways to help people than being a cop."

Chapter Nine

I was running out of time.

The fast approach of graduation loomed in the short distance like a flashing warning sign on a dark, rain-slick night, and I still didn't know what to do—or where or how.

Over the next few weeks I spent a lot of time praying and seeking and trying to figure it out, but up until the day of graduation I still had no idea.

Should I go into law enforcement or ministry?

I just didn't know. And I knew I needed to. At times I felt more strongly pulled to one than the other, but mostly they pulled at me with equal persistence and pressure.

It was time to do something, but what?

I thought about what Frank Morgan had said, how I could help a lot of people as a cop. All the while Dad kept telling me the same thing, telling me how much good I could do and what a waste it would be for me to do anything else, how not using the gifts God had given me as an investigator would be sinful somehow.

But as it turned out, it was Mama Monroe who had been most prescient on the subject.

"Don't limit God," she had said. "Don't think you got to be this or that, fit here not there, all or nothin'. You just trust and obey. God will make a way."

And the way came, like so many things back then, through my connection to and obsession with the Atlanta Child Murders.

The morning of my high school graduation, I was re-reading the case files I had compiled, trying to look again with fresh eyes and a new perspective to see if a new pattern might emerge, if something might leap off the page that before had remained hidden, camouflaged among all the other words and witness statements, details and descriptions.

And as I did, it was as if, once again, I woke up, woke up this time to a new possibility that wasn't either or, all or nothing, but a way to begin to integrate the two seeming disparate callings I was sensing in my soul.

What appeared, what pounced off the page and seized me, was the possibility of simultaneously taking steps to be educated and trained in ministry while working on the case that had captured my imagination, altered my path, haunted my childhood, changed my life.

It happened as I reread and reconsidered the information I had on Curtis Walker.

Thirteen-year-old Curtis Walker was reported missing on February 19, 1981.

He was last seen, wearing a brown-and-blue shirt, blue pants, and blue sneakers, on Bankhead Highway near where he lived in Bowen Homes.

Around this time, Earl Paulk, pastor of Chapel Hill Harvester Church in Decatur, began receiving phone calls from a man claiming to be the killer.

He described himself as a twenty-eight-year-old married man and father of a small child. He said he lured the victims into his blue van by posing as a painter and offering money for part-time work, and claimed responsibility for four of the murders, saying a voice tells him to kill. "Once the voice begins controlling me," he said, "I have no control at all."

The killer claimed he had help, that someone was assisting him in each case.

Following one of the phone calls, the man had agreed to meet with Paulk at his church but never showed. Later, Paulk was told that while he waited in his office for the man, two church elders saw a blue van pull up across the street, hesitate, then drive off.

According to Paulk, two police cars were just coincidentally in the neighborhood, which led him to publicize the call in the hopes that the man would realize he had not been part of a trap.

On February 14th, Paulk issued a televised plea for the killer to turn himself in.

"I work as a church man, a pastor," Paulk said. "I will not set up a trap." He went on to quote the caller saying nobody loved him, nobody had ever loved him, not even his own mother.

The pastor said he believed the man wanted to be free, wanted to be caught. He said the man seemed frightened that the voices would come back to haunt him, that he not only felt controlled by them but was afraid of them.

On March 6th, the body of Curtis Walker was discovered floating face down, snagged on a log in the South River at Waldrop Road less than a mile from Paulk's church.

All Walker's clothes were missing except his underwear, and latent prints were found on his body. The cause of death was ruled asphyxiation by strangulation.

On March 10th, the man called Paulk again. This time the caller discussed four killings, referring to them as the first three and the last one, Curtis Walker, who he mentioned by name.

My mind, like my heart, burst into flames.

I thought of all the possibilities.

What if Pastor Paulk had been contacted by the actual killer? What if it had been a copycat, the person responsible for some if not all of the victims who shouldn't have been on the list or ones who never were?

Was he fixated on the pastor? Would he call him again? Was he a member of his congregation?

That last one stopped me.

Flipping through the files, searching for cases similar to Walker's, I dialed the church.

And that's when the next step in my path was revealed.

I was transferred to a young man named Randy Renfroe, who told me the church was starting a school of ministry in the fall.

By the time I hung up the phone, I was registered for classes at Earl Paulk Institute.

I would move to Atlanta, go to Chapel Hill Harvester Church, attend classes at EPI, studying and preparing for and engaging in ministry, while investigating the Atlanta Child Murders.

I sat there awestruck.

What just happened?

In the course of a single call everything had changed again.

A path had been revealed. A way made plain.

The wait and worry and was over, the ambiguity and indecision departed.

My adventures in ministry and murder investigation were finally about to begin.

Chapter Ten

"Think about what you're saying," Dad said.

"I am," I said. "I have."

"For what? All of an afternoon?"

I didn't say anything, just shook my head.

He had found me in my room packing my things, boxing books, folding clothes into a suitcase.

It had taken four boxes just to hold my case files.

When he asked why, I told him.

Back then he wore a uniform—even on Saturdays, even to his son's high school graduation.

"I just came to see if you were ready for graduation and you drop this on me?" he said.

"It can't be surprising."

"That you're moving to Atlanta? Leaving tonight? Well, it is."

Without the maps and photographs and photocopied scraps of evidence and information tacked to the wall, the room looked abandoned, barren, the white painted sheetrock walls now pocked with a million tiny holes, sad, lonely, looking like the scatter shot from a shotgun.

"You know I've wanted to move to Atlanta, to . . . work the case."

"But that's not what you're talkin' about doin'. It's nearly a year before you can get certified to be a deputy. But you're not even talkin' about that. You're talkin' about . . . what . . . Bible college. It's crazy."

"It's right. It's . . . the next step for me. I know it."

"Well, I don't."

"And?"

"What do you mean *and*?"

I was not being disrespectful in any way, but I wasn't backing down either.

Unlike my brother Jake and my sister Nancy, I had never really had any conflict with either of my parents. I had always been more or less deferential, even submissive, never defiant or disrespectful—especially to Dad.

"I'm the one who has to figure out my next step and take it."

"And you think it's uprooting your entire life, running away?"

"I'm not running away."

Was he confusing me with Nancy? She had run away. To New York. To escape. Two years before and she hadn't written or called or returned or reached out in any way. She had utterly rejected our family. Did he think I was doing the same?

"I'm just going to college," I said. "Just taking the next step in my journey. Nothing more. It's time. It's what we've been planning on. It's just college."

"It's not," he said. "It's not even a real college. It's a new upstart Bible school. It's not even accredited. It's a joke. You can't really believe it's what you're supposed to do."

"I do," I said.

His disappointment was palpable, the force of it powerful. We were in, for us, uncharted territory and it threatened to dampen my joy and excitement.

"Dad," I said, my voice peaceful and placating, "I know it doesn't make any sense but I also know it's what I'm supposed to do."

"It's a mistake."

"I don't think so," I said, "but even if it is, it's one I've got to make."

"It's my job to keep you from making mistakes," he said.

I shook my head. "Not anymore."

"What? You're suddenly all grown up and independent because you're graduating from high school?"

"I just meant—"

"I can't let you do this," he said.

"*Let me*?"

"I won't. I can't."

"Dad, it doesn't have to be this way. Please. Don't make it something that it's not."

"I won't be a part of this," he said. "I told you I'd help with college, but not this one. I won't pay a single dime toward this . . . this impulsive error in judgment. I can't."

I nodded. "Okay."

"I'm sorry, but you'll thank me one day. Take some time to think about some real options. Like Gulf Coast or FSU. We'll talk tomorrow about those. I'll—"

"I won't be here," I said. "I'm leaving tonight."

"You can't. How will you pay for—"

"I'll figure something out," I said. "It'll work out. I believe that. It's all too irrational, illogical, unexpected, and fortuitous not to. But I'd like to at least go with your support."

"Well, I can't give you that."

A lot happened that night. It was another new beginning of sorts. I gained much from the experience, including a new level of autonomy and adulthood, but I lost something too.

I lost some innocence, a sense of home and belonging, but most of all I lost a friend.

My relationship with my dad would never be the same again.

Anna was at graduation. It was the first time I'd seen her in several months. Since Nancy had left town and she had started college we had fallen out of touch.

If anyone could keep me from leaving for Atlanta tonight it was her.

Anna was no longer a secret crush. I was in love with her. Profoundly and absolutely.

It wasn't infatuation or mere attraction, though she was the most beautiful girl in all the world to me. It was unequivocal adoration. A love only a poet could hope to understand. I loved every cell and every second of her, every moment and every molecule.

Of course, not being a poet myself, I was unable to tell her, unable to express the fire for her smoldering inside my chest.

And she had come to graduation with her new boyfriend whose sister was in my class, and I avoided her, quickly ducking out of the gymnasium at the eternal event's conclusion.

Following pomp and circumstance—or all the pomp and circumstance that could be mustered for forty-two graduates, I loaded my car and filled my tank using some of my graduation gift cash at the only convenience store in Pottersville.

After a tearful goodbye at which my mom smelled of booze and from which my dad was absent, I set out for the city too busy to hate, the birthplace of my hero and spiritual mentor Martin Luther King, Jr., who was killed the same year I was born, the home of Coca-Cola, the CDC, CNN, the Carter Center, America's baseball team, the Varsity, Stone Mountain, the Fox Theater, where Lynyrd Skynyrd's famous live version of "Free Bird" on *One More from the Road* was recorded, the place where *Gone with the Wind* had been written, and a series of murders had been committed that had affected me as profoundly as any single event in my entire life.

I drove nearly all night.

Sipping Dr. Pepper and munching on Combos, I sang until my voice grew hoarse with Rick Springfield, John Cougar, Steve Camp, Steve Taylor, Boz Scaggs, Robert Palmer, Russ Taff, Lionel Richie, Hall and Oats, and Phil Collins.

I sang to stay awake. I sang to celebrate. I sang to forget. I sang until I couldn't picture the look of disappointment on my dad's face or the look of happiness on Anna's.

I spent some more of my grad gift money on a cheap motel room. And at nine o'clock the next morning, after only a few hours of sleep, I was walking into the exciting, integrated mega church whose pastor a killer had called, where less than a mile away the small body of Curtis Walker had been found.

Chapter Eleven

"I hear very good things about what you're doing for the kingdom of God," Earl Paulk said. "We're so pleased you chose our school of ministry. I truly believe we've got the resources to equip our students to touch the world."

We were in his upstairs office in the back of the K Center or main sanctuary, a large building he had described as an airplane hanger, built to accommodate as many people as possible due to the growth the church had experienced over the past decade.

What would become Chapel Hill Harvester Church began in December 1960 in Saint John's Lutheran Church on Euclid Avenue, in the Little Five Points community. The thirty-nine people in attendance included founders Earl and Norma Paulk, Don and Clariece Paulk, and Harry and Myrtle Mushegan.

From the first day, Paulk was committed to opening the doors of his church to all people, regardless of racial, economic, or moral background. Not surprisingly, given his opposition to segregation, he was one of the first white pastors to open the doors of his church to black members.

The very first bulletin cover showed a picture of a white hand and a black hand clasped together with the accompanying slogan A Church of Compassion.

The church moved to South Dekalb County in Decatur

in 1972, and quickly became one of the first truly racially integrated congregations in the entire South.

The early eighties witnessed a shift in ministry and message, and explosive growth.

In addition to its unique racial unity, the church became famous for its worship style, which combined visual arts with liturgy, and its social outreach programs.

In 1982, Paulk was ordained as a bishop in the International Communion of Charismatic Churches. His public housing ministry was named one of a thousand points of light by President George H. W. Bush.

I had never been much of a churchgoer and had little use for organized religion, but I appreciated many aspects of this unique, inspiring church, especially the integration, emphasis on compassion, and the social outreach programs to the poor and disenfranchised.

It had taken me a while to get an appointment with Bishop Paulk. I had been in town a few weeks, getting settled, getting my bearings, getting a job.

"I understand you're working for us too?" he said.

I nodded.

Don Paulk, Earl's brother and co-pastor of the church, had been particularly helpful to me, welcoming, supportive, and had even found me a job on the janitorial staff of the facilities department.

"That's great," he said. "Pastor Don's very impressed with you. Says you'll soon be leading a covenant community group."

Covenant communities were the church's home meetings, small groups scattered throughout the city.

"I look forward to it."

There was a presence about Bishop Paulk, an energy emanating from him, particularly from his mesmerizing bright blue eyes. He was trim and fit and sat upright behind his enormous desk. At sixty, his forceful bearing and youthful vitality were extraordinary.

"God's got his hand on your life," he said. "I sense a powerful calling."

"Thank you," I said. "I'm very excited to be here."

Thanks to Pastor Don waving part of the tuition, I was already enrolled in summer classes. In addition to the classes, I had been assigned a practicum that involved, among other things, taking food and medicine into an extremely low-income apartment complex and regular visits to Grady hospital to see a man with AIDS in the last days of his short life.

And all of it—the transition from small to big town, the new job, the classes, the work of actually helping people in need—was exhilarating and exhausting.

I longed to share everything that was happening with Dad and Anna. Being unable to tinged the edges of everything with a certain ever-present, dull-ache sadness.

"Don said you plan to combine ministry and law enforcement somehow."

"I don't know how exactly or if I even can, but I feel equally called to both."

He nodded. "That's what we need. We have too many ministers limiting what they can be, spending all their time in a pulpit. I think you're right on track. Don't limit God. Just stay open to the Holy Spirit. Let me know any way we can help you."

"Pastor Don said you might be willing to talk to me about the child murders that happened a few years back."

He nodded.

"I'll never forget it," he said with a heavy sigh. "So many black parents in our congregation . . . wondering if *their* child would be next. We began a round-the-clock prayer vigil early on but became publicly involved when I received a call from Dr. Frazier Ben Todd—he was president of the NAACP at the time.

"On February fourteenth—this was back in eighty-one—I made a television appeal to the killer or killers and ran a full-page advertisement in the *Atlanta Journal-Constitution* that said, 'If you are responsible for the crimes against our children, this television appeal is to you. Watch Saturday, February 14th, Channel 46 at 11:00 p.m.'

"I assured the killer that he could speak to me in private and I ended by saying, 'Jesus loves you and He will forgive you for what you have done.'

"The very next day, phone calls began coming in from supposed killers. On February sixteenth a mysterious caller instructed me to go to a local TV station for the six o'clock evening news broadcast. The person didn't show but later called saying, 'I didn't see you on camera.' The following Sunday afternoon, I was asked to speak to a city-wide prayer meeting held at the request of the NAACP.

"The day after that a call came in from someone calling himself 'the one Earl Paulk was trying to reach.' I rushed to the phone but when he heard my voice he hung up. He called back an hour later but refused to set a time and place to meet.

"The same voice called later and told us to look for a particular van and when it would arrive. Don and I waited in our car and saw a van matching the description drive into the parking lot across the street from our church. Another car pulled into the lot. I don't know if it was the FBI or police or what. Then two more and suddenly the van spun its wheels and disappeared, moving too fast for us to get a tag number. The two cars didn't pursue so I guess their pulling in when they did was just coincidence."

As I listened to him recount his story I realized there were differences in what I had read and thought from what he remembered, and it occurred to me that it must be that way with every report, every statement, everything I knew or thought I did.

"When he called the next time, he asked us to come to a

truck stop at the edge of town. Don went with me. There were cars everywhere when we arrived. If the caller came he had apparently panicked and left.

"After that, FBI agents surrounded the church property and told us they would be monitoring our phone conversations.

"On February twenty-eighth, I made another television appeal and the caller spoke to me for the last time.

"On March sixth, the next victim was found in a creek about a mile from here.

"A few months after that, Wayne Williams was arrested and eventually convicted, but I've always believed there was more than one killer at work."

"Was there anything that made you think the caller might be a member of your congregation?"

He shrugged. "I never had a knowing one way or another but I don't think he was. He may have attended a service at some point . . . but . . ."

"And you were never contacted again?"

He shook his head. "Not by that person."

"Others?"

"I get calls all the time. A few others have claimed to be involved."

"Any recently?"

He nodded.

"One who called recently said he enjoyed my sermon from the previous Sunday and even quoted from it."

"Could he have seen it on TV?"

"It hadn't aired yet."

I nodded and thought about it, excitement arcing through me.

"You know who you should talk to . . ." he said. "There's a lady in our congregation who runs a daycare. She's been part of STOP since the beginning. Her son was one of the victims who didn't make the list."

Chapter Twelve

Ida Williams owned and operated a daycare and aftercare center called Safe Haven just down Flat Shoals Road from the church.

It was located in a converted home that had been retrofitted and zoned commercial. The large yard, now a playground, was filled with swings and sandboxes and toys, surrounded by a chain-link fence.

I pulled up, parked to one side of the circular driveway, and got out.

By the time I reached the gate, a uniformed security guard was waiting for me.

He was a rotundish, pale man with short blond hair cut in a military-style side-part, and a neatly trimmed blond mustache. His smallish light blue eyes blinked so often behind his glasses they seemed hooded.

"How can I help you?" he asked.

"I'm here to see Ida Williams," I said.

"Have an appointment?"

I shook my head.

"You'll need to make one before she can see you. She's with her kids now. Will be 'til eight. Maybe later."

"But—"

He shook his head. "Sorry. No exceptions."

"I've just—"

"I'm gonna need you to leave the premises, sir. Now."

When he raised his hands, I could see a bright orange Swatch watch stretched around his thick right wrist. It looked odd and out of place and as if at any moment the band would snap and it would slingshot off.

"Can you just tell me—"

"I won't tell you again."

I wondered what he would do instead of telling me again, but an intervening angel prevented me from finding out.

"What is it, Ralph?" she asked.

Small enough to be a schoolgirl. Shy green eyes. Straight sun-streaked blond hair. Smooth, unvarnished, suntanned skin. A simple, understated, graceful beauty I found irresistible.

I knew no one could make me forget Anna, but this alluring, vulnerable, pretty woman-child creature came as close as any to making me believe it was possible.

"No appointment," he said. "Refusing to leave."

"I'm not refusing to leave," I said to her. "I was just trying to explain that Bishop Paulk sent me over and to find out how to go about making an appointment."

"What'd you need?" she asked.

"Just to talk to Ms. Williams for a few minutes."

"Well, you can certainly do that," she said. "I'll take care of it, Ralph."

"Yes, ma'am. I'll radio and let her know you two are coming up."

Ralph opened the gate and I walked through.

"I'm Jordan Moore," she said, extending her small, cold hand.

I smiled. "Really? I'm John Jordan."

She smiled but looked a bit embarrassed, her face and neck blushing crimson.

"Sorry my hands are cold," she said. "Ninety-degree weather and my extremities are little blocks of ice."

She ushered me up the covered walkway and we fell in step beside one another.

"And sorry about Ralph," she said. "He means well. I'm sure you can tell . . . security is taken very seriously around here."

I wondered if she had used the passive voice—*is taken* instead of *we take*—because she found the measures a little extreme.

"It's sort of our speciality," she said.

"Bishop Paulk mentioned Ms. Williams had a son who was killed."

"Changes everything," she said.

We walked in silence for a few moments.

I was young and what I did next had never occurred to me to do before.

When she was looking away, I stole a quick glance at her left hand ring finger, but what I saw gave me questions not answers.

The small, thin, elegant finger held no ring, but it did bear the white, untanned mark where one had recently been.

"How long have you worked here?" I asked.

"Seems like all my life," she said. "I've lost track."

"Tell me about it."

"Daycare during the day. Aftercare in the afternoon and evening. An emphasis on a safe, positive environment. Clean. Accredited. Family owned and operated. It's not affiliated with the church but most of us go there. And most of our kids are from there."

To our right, beyond another fence, the playground was empty, the sun glinting off its shiny surfaces, a swing squeaking as it emptily back-and-forthed in the breeze.

"Where are the kids?" I said. "Figured they'd be on the playground this time of day."

"Finishing up an art project," she said. "They'll be out here" —she looked at her watch— "in four minutes. In fact, we can have a seat here and wait on Miss Ida to come out."

She nodded toward a plastic-mesh-covered metal bench and we sat down.

"Do you go to Chapel Hill?" she asked.

"Came to attend EPI. Just moved here a few weeks ago."

"How do you like Atlanta?"

"Haven't seen much of it yet," I said. "But I like it here. A lot. I'm from a small town in the Florida Panhandle of about a tenth of the size of the church."

"Really?" she asked in surprise. "You don't seem . . ."

"What?"

She shrugged. "I don't know."

"Yes you do. What were you going to say?"

"Small town. You don't seem that small town."

I smiled and she blushed again.

"I'm as small town as John Cougar Mellencamp."

We sat in silence a moment as I tried to work up my nerve to ask her out.

"You lived here long?" I asked.

"My whole life."

"I could use someone to see the city with," I said. "Show me around. Play tour guide. Would you like to—"

"I can't," she said. "Sorry. Let me go see what's keeping Miss Ida."

Chapter Thirteen

Ida Williams—Miss Ida to the kids in her care and the staff that adored her—was a heavy middle-aged black woman with beautiful, smooth skin, big, bright eyes, and brown lips only a shade or two lighter than the rest of her.

Her hair was up in a colorful head wrap of orange and brown and green that matched the large, loose tunic dress she was wearing.

We were seated on the same bench Jordan and I had been on. In front of us, visible through the rings in the fence, children ran and climbed and swung and jumped and talked and laughed, each of them, in one way or another, resembling the victims on the list.

And those not on the list.

Like so many others, LaMarcus Williams never made the list. As in the case with the others, I wasn't sure why. Neither was his mom.

How did she do it? How did she see them every day, day after day, these little fresh faces that looked so much like the son who would never grow old, never become any of what he might have been, never come home again?

"Nothin' in this world like losing a child," she said. "You's not much more'n a child yourself, but if you were older and had a child of your own, you still wouldn't know what I's talkin' about. I didn't. Saw all these grievin' mamas. Felt bad for 'em. Real bad. Thought 'cause I had a kid I knew what they's goin' through. Didn't have a clue."

I nodded but knew better than to say anything. There was nothing *to* say, no words in the history of all words to utter.

"They's nothin' like it, nothin' come close," she said. "But what make it even worse is not knowing, not knowing who did it and why, not knowing if his name should be on that list or not."

Across the playground, Jordan was watching a group of girls jump rope. She was one of only a handful of white faces and the only worker who was in the yard. It may have just been me imagining or wanting, but I thought I saw her looking my way occasionally, even turning red and smiling once when our eyes met.

"That's why I can't quit, can't give up," she said. "People say the man in jail, the murders stopped. Time to let go, move on."

I understood why she couldn't, why she would never be able to. At least not until—it was at that moment that I decided to dedicate myself to finding out what happened to LaMarcus Williams.

"I joined STOP even before my boy was taken from me," she said. "Been workin' 'long side Camille and Willie Mae and all the others all these years. Seen lots of people come and go."

STOP was the name used by the committee of mothers formed to stop children's murders. It began when three of the victims' mothers, Camille Bell, Willie Mae Mathis, and Venus Taylor, joined with Reverend Earl Carroll to bring attention to Atlanta, to the slaughter of the innocent, the ineffectiveness of the police, and the indifference of too many in the white power establishment.

"They's a group of us still meets every week," she said.

"Every single week."

"May I come to it?" I asked. "I'd like to get involved."

She nodded. "It's open to anyone. Meet right here every Thursday night."

"I'll be here. Thank you."

"There's also a support group at the church," she said. "For anyone who's lost a child. It's a closed group, but you can come as my guest if you like."

"I would. Thank you."

She turned and looked down across Flat Shoals Road at the K Center and Chapel Hill's other facilities, her first time taking her eyes off the children.

"Not sure I'd've made it without them," she said. "The Paulks. They were all so good to me. Bishop. Don and Clariece. Still are, but I mean when it happened . . . they kept me from going crazy. Them and my daughter. I had lost my husband the year before. It was just . . . too . . ."

"Do you . . . mind . . . would you . . . be willing to tell me what happened?"

Her watchful gaze was back on the children.

"Happened right here," she said. "Wasn't a daycare then. Was our home. Saturday after Thanksgiving. November twenty-ninth."

I was here at that same time, I thought. Safely tucked away inside the Omni with my family while she was losing everything.

"He was only twelve," she said. "Just a twelve-year-old little boy."

We had been the same age, would still be had he not been cut loose from whatever it is that tethers us here.

"Out in the yard playing," she said. "The backyard. Away from the road. Back where nobody could get to him, back where I could see him. I was back and forth between the living room and kitchen, cooking supper and wrapping his Christmas presents. A Star Wars lunchbox. Guess Who game. GI Joe. Star

Trek Communicators. Rubik's Cube. Train set. Michael Jackson and Kool and the Gang records. Spent too much. Didn't care. Was so happy I found them. Both rooms had big windows that looked out over the backyard. I watched him like a hawk. Always had, but once our children started bein' taken . . . I never took my eyes off of him."

But she had, hadn't she? For a moment, a split second, maybe a little longer.

She was still looking at the children before us, but I wondered what she was really seeing.

"I didn't think I had . . . I don't remember not seeing him for even a moment—least out the corner of my eye. But . . . one moment he was there, another he was gone. Just vanished. Gone. Just like that. Never saw my boy alive again."

She was crying now. Still looking straight ahead as tears streamed down her dark, round cheeks.

"I's the reason he's out there," she said. "I wanted to wrap his gifts I had just gotten the day before and get 'em up under the tree. I sent him out there. I did. I'm the reason my boy's dead."

Chapter Fourteen

EPI was too new and too small to have dormitories, so school housing was a three-story apartment in Trade Winds Apartment Complex up off Wesley Chapel Road near I-20.

My new address was 4636 Pleasant Point Drive, my home, a drug-ridden, rundown low-income complex where I shared an apartment designed for a family of four with eight testosterone-ridden late-teen men, only about half of whom were actually attending EPI. The others were single young men from the church who needed a place to live.

Many of the students complained about the living conditions at Trade Winds, the shape of the property itself, the makeup of those who called it home, but I loved it. As a young white man from a tiny town in Florida, I was an outsider and part of a small minority. I was surrounded by mostly poor African-Americans and I had never felt more at home, more at ease, never before felt more in the center of exactly where I was supposed to be, doing what I was supposed to be doing.

Of course, the truth was I had always felt more at home around Merrill and his mom and their family and friends and the black woman who had kept me as a child than I had nearly anyone else.

I had undergone a sea change long before coming to Atlanta and was now undergoing another. Not only had I gone from a small North Florida town with one traffic light to the eight-lane interstates of a crowded metropolitan area, but I had left behind my virtually solitary existence, so comfortable to my essentially introverted nature, for a crowded, close community where I was surrounded by people—lots and lots of them—nearly every waking moment of every single day.

In the mornings on my way to class, I'd stop in the little doughnut shop on Wesley Chapel for maple and strawberry iced doughnuts. In the evenings, I'd go through the drive-thru of the Dairy Queen. Both were within a block of Trade Winds and made up in convenience and cost for what they lacked in taste and variety.

This afternoon I came home without grabbing my usual chicken sandwich and fries. Hearing Ida Williams's heartbreaking account of what happened to her son left me without an appetite and with a sharp need to spend some extra time with the best friend I'd made in the city so far, my little neighbor basketball buddy, Martin Fisher.

Martin was the age LaMarcus had been when age ceased to be something he could be measured by, the age I had been when I had confronted Wayne Williams—something I had done just twenty short minutes from where we stood right now.

Martin was small and scrawny for his age, often sick. Chronic untreated ear infections as a small child had left him almost completely deaf and with a pretty severe speech impediment.

Martin's monotone voice was nasally and guttural and difficult for most people to understand, but we had spent so much time together we had very little trouble communicating.

We both loved basketball and met each afternoon on the small asphalt court in the center of the complex.

The backboards were metal and the old, oblong goals were canted and netless.

"Yon, Yon," Martin yelled, "I . . . 'm . . . o'en."

He was dancing around under the goal with his hands up, imploring me to pass him the ball.

"Of course you're open," I said. "Nobody here but us. Move around. Post up. Get in a good position. Catch the ball. Gather. Go up strong. Ready?"

"'een 'eady."

I bounce-passed him the ball.

He tried to shoot too quickly, before he even had the ball, and lost it as he went up.

"You've got to catch it first," I said. "Catch it. Gather yourself. Go up strong."

"I 'ow," he said. "I 'ot 'is. Do it a'ain."

We did the same thing again. We got the same results.

The next time, he caught and gathered, but was too small and weak to get the ball up over the rim.

"Practice the right form," I said. "Elbow straight, arch the ball, follow through. Doesn't matter if it doesn't go in. Just shoot it the right way."

"It 'oes 'atter, Yon," he said.

I shook my head, took a dribble and then a step-back jumper from about twenty feet.

He squealed when it fell through the rim without touching anything until it hit the asphalt below.

"Get your form right now," I said. "Size and strength will come later."

I passed him the ball and he began dribbling. Unable to dribble between his legs, he lifted one and went under it to approximate the same move.

"What's for 'inner 'oonight, Yon?"

I didn't know a lot about Martin's situation, had no idea what life was like for him once the apartment door closed behind him. He lived in the unit directly next to ours and I had seen several people come and go, but had yet to identify or meet anyone who would pass for parents.

Of the little I had been able to gather, two constants had emerged. He seemed to never be supervised and to always be hungry.

Lately, we had been taking to the kitchen to find something to feed him following our hoop exploits.

"Whatta you want?" I asked. "You can have fish sticks or I could whip up some fish sticks."

He laughed. "Yon," he said, holding out the ball.

Since I rarely cooked, I kept very little food in what was the community kitchen of the EPI dorm apartment, but after Martin identified them as his favorite, I had maintained a large bag of fish sticks in the small freezer.

"You decide buddy," I said. "It's up to you."

"'ish sticks," he shouted.

"Okay," I said. "Make ten layups on each side and we'll adjourn to the kitchen."

As he began his layup attempts, Frank Morgan pulled up in an unmarked.

I smiled. I had called his office and left a message but had not told him where I was living.

As Martin worked on his layups, I walked over to where Frank was parking.

"How'd you find me?" I asked as he got out of the car.

"Only white face in Trade Winds," he said. "Wasn't hard."

"Haven't see a lot of those in here," I said toward his car.

"Kind we send in here are far more unmarked," he said. "The hell you doin' livin' in a place like this?"

I told him.

"Your dad says y'all aren't speaking."

"I'm speaking. Just not doing exactly what he wants me to right now. Pretty much a first. Least on anything that really mattered to him."

"We've got a spare bedroom," he said. "Welcome to it long as you like."

"Thank you. That means a lot. But this is where I'm supposed to be."

All around us the desultory sounds of poverty, of idleness, of listlessness, and waste, rose and fell, ebbed and flowed, sat still and swelled.

Grown men gathered around conversations of no consequence. They had no job, no purpose, nowhere to be. Women too-early old sitting on front door stoops, fanning themselves, watching the world spin by, spin away from them. Always away. Young men working in vain on vehicles that would never run again. Other, younger young men dealing substances to escape the disappointment and misery. Competing radios and game shows on too-loud TVs.

Ragged, rundown buildings around an asphalt parking lot dotted with a billion black stains from careless spills, discarded trash, and oil-leaking low riders, waves of shimmering heat rising up from all of them in the suffocating, will-breaking afternoon sun.

Martin continued attempting layups, his lack of success not from lack of effort or enthusiasm.

"When'd you adopt him?" Frank asked.

I laughed.

He shook his head. "Looks an awful lot like the little faces on the list."

He was right. He did. I hadn't consciously made the connection. Why hadn't I? What was my subconscious up to?

"Speaking of . . ." I said. "Why didn't LaMarcus Williams make the list?"

He smiled knowingly. "There it is. *That's* why you called."

"Yon, Yon," Martin yelled when he finally got one to go. "You 'ee 'at?"

"I did. Very nice. Keep it up. Just like that. Same way every time."

"LaMarcus Williams," Frank said. "That's the kid

snatched out of his backyard on Flat Shoals. Too much was different from the others to make the list."

"There are a lot of differences between the ones that made the list."

"Told you. The list is arbitrary."

"Forget the girls and adults," I said. "Forget all but the true pattern cases of asphyxiated young boys. LaMarcus fits their profile, right? Why'd they make the list and he didn't?"

"He wasn't a poor inner city street kid. He was snatched from his backyard. He wasn't taken far. Found pretty soon after he was killed. And there were differences in the way he was killed. Can't remember what exactly, but . . ."

"Were there suspects? Was Williams looked at for it after he became the prime suspect in the other cases?"

"That I can't tell you," he said.

"Can you put me in touch with the lead detective on the case?"

He nodded. "That I can do."

Chapter Fifteen

"We ain't much," Ida Williams said. "But we are faithful."

I knew where the faithfulness came from. I knew why this small group continued to meet some four years after Wayne Williams was sentenced to serve two life sentences. They had seen what a small group of passionate people could do. If not for the three victims' mothers—Camille Bell, Willie Mae Mathis, and Venus Taylor—forming STOP and pressuring the police, politicians, and the white power structure, who knows how long it would have taken for a task force to be formed.

"Mule headed more like it," Melvin, a large black man, said.

"We surely are that," Ida agreed.

The gathering of the faithful took place in the back corner of the Safe Haven daycare center and included Ida, Melvin, a tall, thin woman named Rose Lee, a squat, muscular, fireplug of a man named Preston Mailer, and to my delight and surprise Jordan Moore.

Mailer was a retired cop. He along with everyone but me and Jordan were black.

"Wanna welcome our new member," Ida said. "This is John Jordan. He's new to Atlanta but has been followin' the case a long time. He'll be a real asset to the group."

"Thank you for havin' me," I said. "I've been interested and invested in this case since childhood and I look forward to being involved in the work y'all are doin'."

"By way of introducin' John to our group and for us to hear from him, I thought we'd do one of our round robin brainstorm sessions tonight," Ida said.

Everybody indicated their assent.

"We learn by sharin', by aksin' questions—of each other and ourselves. Nobody got to agree with anybody on anything. Only rule is be courteous."

"That means you, Preston," Rose Lee said.

"Never been anything but," he said.

"Anything but a butt," she said.

It was said in good humor and everyone laughed.

"We're a diverse group, John," Ida said. "Some believe Wayne Williams was set up, that he's completely innocent."

Preston raised his hand.

"Some think he's guilty of all twenty-nine on the list plus some."

Rose Lee raised her hand and smiled.

"Others, like myself and Jordan, think it possible Wayne Williams did some of 'em but just as possible he didn't. We just ain't convinced either way. What we think more likely is if he did 'em, he didn't do 'em all."

I nodded.

"Why don't we start with what John thinks," Jordan said.

"Good idea," Ida said. "John?"

"I don't know," I said. "I've studied and studied the case against Wayne Williams—and I've had access to a lot of task force documents and information the general public hasn't—but I just—"

"How?" Preston Mailer asked.

"Let the young man talk, Preston," Ida said.

"How what?" I asked.

"How'd you get task force documents and information?"

Preston Mailer was a large, fleshy, light-skinned black man with thinning and receding gray hair on top of his huge head. His thick, swollen-looking skin was the color of river clay, a hint of red hue in it, his face dotted with dark freckles and moles the size and shape of the small black specks deposited in the filter of a faucet connected to an old copper pipe.

"My dad's in law enforcement," I said. "We had a friend on the task force."

"Who?"

I shook my head. "Won't tell you that."

He huffed, frowning and shaking his enormous head.

"So you've had access to this information the general public doesn't have . . ." Jordan said.

"And I still don't know. I go back and forth. Sometimes I think in spite of the weak case against Williams, he really is the killer—the main serial killer who killed with a certain pattern. Other times I think he's innocent of not only what he was charged with but the other murders as well. The fibers are compelling . . . but there are some problems with them."

"Such as?" Preston said.

"Trace evidence—hair and fibers and other substances exchanged during contact—should work both ways. Hair from Williams's dog and fibers from his carpet shouldn't just be found on the victims, but some of their hair and fibers should've been found on him—or in his home or car."

Everyone nodded, including Preston.

"There are other problems too," I said. "The fibers they found on some of the victims and tied to Williams aren't as rare as the prosecution claimed. And in at least one case, the prosecution matched fibers found on one of the victims to a car the Williams didn't own at the time."

I had everyone's attention, but most enjoyed Jordan's.

"What about there not being such a thing as a black serial killer?" Preston said.

"That's been the conventional wisdom," I said, "but it's just not true. There have been others before Williams and the more data the FBI gets, the more they see it's far more common than anyone knew."

He shook his head. "I don't buy it. Serial killers are white males, eighteen to thirty-five."

"Most are," I said. "But not all."

"What else?" Jordan said. "Keep on."

Was she reconsidering going out with me? She was certainly responding to me in a way she hadn't before.

"You started by saying the fiber evidence is compelling," Rose Lee said.

"It is," I said. "The sheer volume of it is staggering. And that it can link Williams's environment to so many of the victims."

"His environment," Ida said. "Exactly. Did anyone ever look at his dad? Could Homer Williams have committed the crimes?"

"Or Faye?" Jordan said.

"Good questions," I said. "I don't know the answers."

"But what else makes you suspect Wayne Williams?" Rose Lee asked.

"There're a lot of things. I don't put a ton of stock in them, but I don't totally discount the eyewitnesses who testified they saw Williams with some of the victims. The way in which he lies and exaggerates. His behavior in general, but after he began being followed by the police in particular—calling a press conference and the things he said, leading police to the houses of people connected to the case, failing lie detector tests, his interest in law enforcement."

"Which you and I share with him," Preston said.

I nodded. "But we were never busted for impersonating an officer."

"He was?" Jordan asked.

"He was. He also showed up at one of the crime scenes

offering to take pictures for the cops."

"Really?" Preston said. "I didn't know that."

"His outbursts on the witness stand," I continued. "The way he changed so drastically. But more than anything else except the hairs and fibers is the entire bridge incident. During the weeks of river and bridge stakeouts, Williams was the only one to ever be stopped. What was he doing there? Why did he turn around and cross over the bridge again? He lied about what he had done earlier in the evening. It was three o'clock in the morning and the reason he gave for being there was bullshit. He said he had an audition the next morning with Cheryl Johnson and he had driven around trying to verify where she lived and when he couldn't, he went in search of a pay phone. No one, not the police, not the FBI, not the press, not the defense team has ever been able to find this Cheryl Johnson. This was the biggest, highest profile case since . . . maybe ever. You don't think if she existed she would've come forward by now?"

Everyone seemed to be pondering what I was saying—even Preston.

"Then there's the report that a small piece of rope and a change of clothes were found in his station wagon the night he was pulled over on the bridge," I continued. "There were also drops of blood found in the station wagon that were the same type as at least two of the victims. Witnesses say he and his dad were seen burning clothes and papers and other things that could be considered evidence in their backyard once he became a person of interest in the case. And I know a lot of people don't, but I put a lot of stock in the profile—and the fact that the two FBI profilers who worked the case, Roy Hazelwood and John Douglas, believe Williams to be guilty. All that said, I still can't be certain—which probably has more to do with the way the evidence was handled than questions about the evidence itself."

As was often the case, when I finished going through the case against Williams, I was convinced he was responsible for of the killings. Unanswered questions would eventually cause doubt to creep back in, and I would never be convinced he killed everyone on the list, but in that moment I believed him to be the serial killer responsible for the serial killings within the greater list of victims.

"What about the killings that've happened since Wayne was arrested?" Preston said. "How can you explain those?"

"Same way you explain the ones that weren't part of the pattern while Wayne was out," I said. "Someone else is doing them. Probably several someone elses. To me, the serial killer—whether it's Williams or someone else—killed serially, as part of a distinct pattern in a particular way. I'd say the young black males who were asphyxiated were part of that pattern. The others, and there were and still are many, were done by others for other reasons. That means the famous list is wrong. That means that you have to exclude females and adults and the young males who were stabbed or shot. And what you have following Williams's arrest are mostly stabbings and shootings."

"You may be right," Preston said. "But if you are that means the two victims Wayne was actually convicted of killing shouldn't've even been on the list to begin with."

I nodded.

"And that my brother should've been," Jordan said.

"Your brother?" I asked in surprise.

"LaMarcus," she said.

"My boy," Ida said. "She's his sister. Me and her daddy married when the kids were still little."

I nodded.

"So why ain't he?" Ida asked. "Why ain't my son on the list?"

"I don't know," I said, "but it's the first thing I intend to find out."

Chapter Sixteen

"Wow," Jordan said. "You really breathed new life back into our little group."

We were walking down the breezeway after having locked up, the others milling around the parking lot, making sure not to leave her alone with the new member obsessed with murder.

"They're lingering," I said, nodding toward them.

"They're protective," she said.

"I get it," I said. "What they've been through, what they've seen. I'm glad they are."

"They're sweet," she said. "They've been with me through a lot over the years."

"I had no idea LaMarcus was your brother," I said. "I'm so sorry."

"No way you could've known."

The diamond in her wedding set glinted in the light of one of the overhead Fluorescent bulbs.

"I also didn't know you were married when I asked you out," I said. "Sorry. You weren't wearing your ring and . . ."

"Please don't apologize," she said. "It was the kindest, most flattering thing to happen to me in a long time. I take them off at work. They snag on everything."

"The truth is I saw the tan line and asked anyway. I

shouldn't have. I'm sorry."

"That's just an excuse," she said.

"Huh? What is?"

"Work."

"I'm—"

"I don't just take my rings off because they snag," she said. "I . . . I'm . . . It's not your fault. I'm sure you were just pickin' up on . . . my . . . I've said too much already. You're too easy to talk to."

"Please," I said.

"I'm in a situation I've needed to be out of for a very long time," she said. "I just haven't been able to find a way out and . . ."

"And?"

"And I'm sure you were pickin' up on my attraction too. I've never . . . I can't remember it . . . it's never been quite so immediate or . . ."

"Come on, slowpokes," Preston called. "I'm ready to go home."

"Can I give you a ride?" I asked.

"NO," she exclaimed. "Sorry, but . . . that would be the worst thing. Thank you, but . . . I can't. And I really shouldn't talk to you again. I'm sorry. I wish things were different."

Before I could say anything else, we reached the others.

"Good meeting everyone," Ida said. "See you next week."

"So glad you joined us, John," Rose Lee said.

A black Trans Am screeched off the street and into the driveway, racing up to where we stood.

"Oh my God," Jordan said, moving away from me and over by Ida.

"It's okay, Jordan," Ida said. "You're okay, baby."

"He's supposed to be at work."

"Larry Moore," Rose Lee whispered to me, "Jordan's husband."

A smallish but muscular man in very short exercise shorts and a tank top tucked into them jumped out of the car.

His hair was feathered and blown back and he wore a large, flat gold chain around his neck, the bottom of which disappeared into his thick chest hair.

"What the hell, Jordan?" he said. "Why aren't you at home?"

"Our meeting ran a little long," Ida said. "I was just about to take her."

"Get in the car, Jordan," he said. "Now."

She actually shook.

"I . . . I thought . . . you were at work," she said. "I . . . wouldn't've stayed for the meeting. I didn't know."

"My wife out to all hours of the night," he said. "What the hell? Get in the car."

He stopped when he saw me.

"Who the hell is this?"

Ida started to answer, but I stepped forward. "John Jordan," I said.

"You bowing up at me, bitch?" he said.

I didn't respond, just stood there.

"Jordan, get in the fuckin' car now. And wipe your feet."

She moved toward the car. Hesitantly. Slowly. Self-consciously.

"Come home with me, baby," Ida said.

"Stay out of it, Ida," he said. "She's coming home with her husband—where she should've been hours ago."

"She better be at work on time in the morning," Ida said. "And there better not be a mark on her."

Jordan carefully eased into the car, looking like a frightened child.

"Come on, *Mom*, you know I wouldn't do that," he said to Ida. "I never leave marks."

He then jumped into his car and sped away.

"Lord Jesus, the things that poor child done been through," Ida said.

We were walking back toward the building so she could use the phone.

"I know the scriptures say God won't put more on a body than they can bear," she said, "but I don't see how she's still gettin' up of a mornin'."

Everyone else in group had gone—including Preston. I guess he concluded I didn't have the same intentions toward Ida as I did Jordan.

"Can't help but think it's my fault," she said. "I'm the only mama she ever had, the only family for more'n six years now."

"She's lucky to have you."

"Done somethin' wrong, her with a man like that," she said.

Inside, she walked directly to the phone and punched in a number from memory.

"Sorry to bother you so late, Sergeant," she said.

She paused and listened.

"He just picked her up here at the daycare, yellin' and cussin' and showboatin' in his little vroom vroom car."

She paused again.

"Okay. Thank you. Don't know what I'd do if he hurt her again. Okay then. Goodnight."

She hung up and we locked up again.

"Okay," she said, "let's try to go get some sleep. I got to be back here in just a few short hours."

"So Jordan's okay?"

"That was Larry's brother, Vince. Said he'd take care of it. I've had to call him before. He's always handled it."

"You called him *sergeant*."

"He's not just Larry's brother, he's his commanding officer."

"He's in the military?" I asked.

"No," she said, shaking her head. "Larry's a cop."

Chapter Seventeen

I was unable to sleep that night.

All I could think about was Jordan Moore.

I saw her when I closed my eyes. I saw her when I opened them.

Was she okay? How could she be with such a shallow bully loser? Why did he have to be a cop? Why did she have to be so beautiful, so vulnerable, be in such an unbelievably bad situation?

Where was she right now? Locked in the bathroom, Larry beating down the door? Lying uneasily in the bed beside him? Unconscious? Drugged? In the hospital? Dead?

I had no way of contacting her. Didn't know her phone number, address, anything. Nothing I could really do even if I did.

I felt powerless and pathetic, a kid come to the city to uncover a killer and I couldn't even help a helpless woman in danger.

I was so damn helpless myself.

I laid down and tried to sleep but it was futile.

The phone rang a few minutes later.

I answered it in the dark, grabbing the receiver so hurriedly I dropped it, hoping it was Jordan, knowing it couldn't be.

"John?"

It was Anna.

"Hey."

"Did I wake you? I figured you'd be up."

"I am. I was. You didn't wake me."

"Are you okay?"

"Why?"

"You sound . . . I don't know. Is something wrong?"

"I'm okay. How are you? How is Chris?"

"I looked for you after graduation, but . . . I can't believe you moved to Atlanta before I could say goodbye. You Jordans don't mess around gettin' out of town, do you?"

I didn't say anything.

"Speaking of," she said, "you heard anything from Nancy?"

"Not a word."

"She probably doesn't know how to contact you."

"Probably, but she never called when she did, so . . ."

"Guess that's true."

"How'd you find me?"

"I got your number from your mom."

In the darkness of my smallish room there was only the sound of the oscillating fan and Anna's voice.

"Are you mad at me?" she asked. "Did I do something?"

"What would you have done?"

"Nothing to my knowledge."

"I better go," I said. "Thanks for calling."

She sighed.

"You haven't told me how you like Atlanta, how everything's goin', nothin'."

"We'll catch up soon," I said.

"I'm worried about you, John."

"Don't be. Really."

"Can't help it. Feel worse now than before I called."

"Good night, Anna."

"I . . . I love you, John."

After a few hours of tossing and turning, worrying and thinking the worst, I pushed my weary body out of the bed and stumbled down the stairs to the kitchen.

To my surprise, I found Aaron Iris sitting at the rickety old table eating Cap'n Crunch and reading our theology textbook, a tiny trail of milk on the table between the bowl and his mouth.

"John the Revelator," he said.

He was a pudgy, pale-faced freshman with large glasses and strawberry-blond hair, good natured if a bit grating.

"How's it goin' Aaron?"

"I'm too excited to sleep too," he said.

"About?"

"Being here. Being a part of such an amazing movement, learning Kingdom Theology, preparing to take this fresh revelation to the world."

"Oh that," I said.

"Whatta you plan to do?" he said.

"Huh?"

"In ministry. With your life. Where are you called? What are you called to do?"

I shrugged. "No idea."

"Really? I want to be on staff here one day."

"You and every other student in the school."

"You don't?"

I shook my head.

"But there's no other place like this in the whole world, no other man of God like the bishop."

I didn't say anything.

"What?"

"I didn't say anything."

"What're you thinkin'?"

"Something special is happening here," I said. "Truly. And so much of what Bishop Paulk is preaching is—"

"You don't agree with all of it?" he said. "How can you not agree with all of it? What do you have a problem with?"

"I'm just . . . Be careful, man. That's all I'm sayin'. Just be careful not to get so caught up you make idols out of places and people."

"Okay, sure, but I want to know what you disagree with."

"I agree with far more than I disagree with," I said. "I can't tell you how much I appreciate the message of compassion and social justice, community and responsibility."

"But?"

"The message and structure is too authoritarian, too paramilitary in a way," I said. "And too dogmatic. As much as Bishop Paulk is destroying dogmas from previous traditions, he's creating new ones. Maybe all men and movements do it. But it's dangerous."

He shook his head. "Why're you here?"

"What?"

"If you think all that. Why are you here?"

"I guess because the brochure didn't mention there wasn't room for dissent and disagreement."

When I arrived at Safe Haven the next morning, the same security guard met me at the gate with the same demeanor and disposition.

"Deja vu," I said.

"Huh?" he said, blinking behind his glasses.

"We did this same thing a few days ago."

"Did we?" he asked.

"Really?"

"You need to move your car and—"

"It's okay, Ralph," Jordan said, walking up. "He's expected."

Jordan had stopped some ten feet or so back from the

gate and I rushed over to where she was standing.

"Thanks for expecting me."

"Sorry about last night," she said.

She was as radiant as the morning, her simple, unvarnished beauty gently resting on her like a light dew upon the earth. But she appeared to be weary and a bit frazzled too.

"You don't have anything to apologize for."

We starting walking back up toward the building.

Kids were already playing on the playground, their sleepy faces fresh, their drowsy movements measured, less energetic and enthusiastic as they had been when I had seen them before.

"I don't want to cause you any more trouble than you already have," I said, "but I had to make sure you were okay."

"I'm okay. I'm embarrassed, drained, a little sore, and—"

"Did he—"

"Just some shoving and shaking," she said.

"Shoving and shaking is not—"

"Can we not talk about it right now?" she said. "I'm just so happy to see you. Makes everything better. I knew . . . I knew you were the kind . . . I knew you would check on me. I knew I was right about you."

"You were right," I said. "I'm a decent human being."

"You're so much more than that. I can tell."

Our eyes locked.

"Be careful," she said, "or you'll restore my hope in the human race."

"**W**hoever killed LaMarcus Williams took him right here from his backyard with his mom close by," Bobby Battle said. "Wayne Williams never did anything like that. He preyed on street kids who thought *they* were hustlin' *him*."

We were standing behind the daycare center in what was once LaMarcus Williams's backyard.

It was later that afternoon, hot, humid, the sun beating down on us, the rumble of thunder rolling in the far distance.

Bobby Battle, the lead detective in the open unsolved, was walking me through the case, explaining why LaMarcus didn't make the list.

He was roughly the same age and size of Frank Morgan, but that's where the similarities ended. Where Frank wore comfortable, sensible shoes, Sears slacks, a simple cotton button down, and an out-of-date tie, Bobby was stylish and slick, expensively and smartly dressed, more a *Miami Vice* cop than an actual working detective.

"Even still, first thing I did after Williams was arrested was looked at him hard for this," he said. "And I'm not saying he didn't do it. I'm just saying it doesn't fit his pattern."

"You could't rule him out completely?" I asked.

He shook his head. "He had no alibi and check this out—he did come very close to here that same day."

"What?" I asked, my voice rising, pulse quickening.

"Says he was downtown at the Omni passing out flyers for his band."

"He was. I saw him."

"Huh?"

I told him.

"Wow. So there you go, we know where he was earlier in the day. Said when he got asked to leave there he headed down this way."

Did what I had done cause LaMarcus to lose his life?

"Says he came to pick up a piece of recording equipment from a musician who lived about a mile from here."

"Where?"

"Down off Waldrop," he said. "Not far from here."

I experienced a flutter and feeling of excitement and connection, a new feeling then, but one that would happen more and more often over the years, in *ah-ha* moments, in moments when the blurry Polaroid that was my mind would finish developing and come into focus, moments when a few individual puzzle pieces would be laid in place, finally revealing the whole.

"Where Curtis Walker was found three months later," I said.

"Fuck me. That's right. It was the other end but Williams could've picked out the spot when he crossed over the bridge, filed it away for later."

I nodded.

"Goddamn," he said. "That could really be somethin'."

"Question is, did he come over this way before or after that and kill LaMarcus?"

"I just don't think so. According to the mom, she and her daughter, adopted white girl named—has your last name—Jordan, were keeping an eye on the boy while cooking a meal and wrapping Christmas presents. Swears one of 'em had an eye on him every second, but even if that's not true, it was a daring abduction."

I nodded.

It was nap time at Safe Haven. All was quiet, still, peaceful.

The area around the yard was wooded on all three sides.

"Back behind here there's a subdivision," Battle said, pointing with his radio to the trees and undergrowth lining the back of the property. "But when LaMarcus was taken they had just begun the development. Roads and sidewalks were in, a couple of houses under construction, but nobody lived back there."

"So if not Williams, a worker on one of the crews sees LaMarcus at some point," I said. "Starts fixating, fantasizing, planning, watches him from the woods, then snatches him."

"That was one theory. We checked everybody out, assuming we actually found everybody, and came up with two suspects—drywall guy named Vincent Storr and painter named

Raymond J. Pelton."

"And?"

"Both alibied out. Never even found enough to bring 'em in."

"Other suspects?"

"Looked pretty hard at the dad," he said. "Well, the kid's sperm donor. That's about all he ever did for the kid. Anthony Alex Williams, Jr. Sold and installed car stereos. Was mostly a front for dealing. A lady friend said he was givin' her little Anthony all afternoon. Always thought she was lying but never could get her to blink."

"Anyone else?"

"Neighborhood kid. Carlton Fields. Older kid. Not quite right. Not full retarded but . . . Played with the younger kids, including LaMarcus. Parents wouldn't really let us at him and I didn't have any reason to force them to, but . . . I don't know. Always thought there was somethin' there."

"You kept track of 'em over the years?"

"The suspects? Not really. Wish I had time. This ain't the only open unsolved I got, and I got more current cases than I can work effectively."

"I really appreciate you takin' the time to go over it with me."

"No problem. Frank says you're good people. You come up with anything, you bring it to me."

"I will."

"Promise?"

"Promise."

"Then let's take a look at what's really interesting about this case."

Chapter Eighteen

"So," Bobby said, "LaMarcus is playing in his backyard. His mom and sister are watching from the windows. The child murders are high profile by now, so everybody's keepin' an eye on their kids—'specially somebody like Ida Williams, who's part of STOP, right?"

I nodded.

"He's right here where we are," he said. "Fifteen feet from the window. That puts him some twenty feet or more from the wooded border on each side. And then *poof* . . . he's gone. Vanished into thin air."

I looked around the yard. It was still exactly as he was describing.

When I looked at the windows in the back of the house, Ida and Jordan were standing there watching us.

I gave a small wave and frowned apologetically.

They both smiled and waved.

I walked over to the window and Ida opened it.

"I'm sorry about this," I said.

"For trying to find out what happened to my boy?" she said. "Don't be."

"For stirring it up."

"It stays stirred up," Jordan said. "Always. Every single second of every single day."

"We appreciate what you're doing," Ida said.

"How long before the kids go out front to play?" I asked.

"Just a few minutes. Why?"

"Can y'all have someone watch them for a few minutes and help us with something?"

"Sure."

I turned around and took a few steps back toward Bobby.

"Do you mind if we try something?" I asked.

He looked at his watch.

"It will only take a minute."

"Sure." He nodded.

Five minutes later, I was inside the empty daycare center with Ida and Jordan.

The interior walls had been removed when the house was converted into a daycare, but Jordan was seated in approximately the same spot she had been when she was a teenager helping her mother wrap her little brother's Christmas presents. Ida was standing where she had stood.

The windows they were looking out of were exactly the same as they had been on the day LaMarcus disappeared.

Out in the yard, about fifteen feet from the window, a boy about LaMarcus's size was standing, waiting.

Both women had assured me that they were okay with this and they had chosen the best, bravest boy to stand in for LaMarcus. I was still concerned, but my need to know, to see, to get answers was overriding everything else.

"If at any time you want us to stop, just tell me," I said.

"Okay, but we're fine," Ida said. "I promise."

"Okay," I said. "Now, when I say *go*, Ida, I want you to walk from what was the dining room to the kitchen without looking at—without looking through the windows. Jordan, I want you to look down like you're wrapping a present. Don't look up until your mom says *now*. Ida, when you reach what was the kitchen window, I want you to pause just a moment then look up and yell *now*. Okay?"

They both nodded.

I leaned out the window and yelled, "EVERYBODY READY . . . AND . . . GO."

As soon as I yelled *go*, both women did as instructed.

From the wooded area on the right, Bobby Battle ran as fast as he could toward the little LaMarcus stand-in. When he reached him he grabbed him, hoisting him over his shoulder, and began running back to the woods.

He had only taken a few steps when Ida yelled, "NOW."

Jordan looked up. So did Ida. And Bobby with the boy dangling over his shoulder stopped in place.

"Thank you," I said.

Jordan broke down and began to sob.

I walked over to her as Bobby put down our little helper and escorted him to the playground in the front.

"I'm sorry," I said.

"No," Jordan said. "Are you kidding? It's the best thing ever. I always thought if I had just not looked down, not even for a second, LaMarcus would't've been taken."

Back outside with Bobby.

"No way somebody could run in, snatch him, and get out again before being seen," he said.

"Unless—" I began.

"There is no unless."

"Unless both women were distracted by something at the same time that lasted longer than they realize."

"Think of the split-second timing that'd have to be

involved. The chances are slim to none. But add in the killer knowing they were distracted or just happening to do it at that moment . . . It's impossible."

"Unless," I said.

"I'm telling you there is no unless," he said. "Unless what?"

"The killer created the distraction."

He started to say something but stopped. After a moment he smiled. "Suppose it's possible."

"There are probably far more, but I can think of two other possibilities so far," I said.

"Yeah?"

"LaMarcus was playing closer to the woods than they realized," I said. "Both of those scenarios just mean the eyewitnesses only have to be a little off about a relatively small point."

He shook his head. "Never known an eyewitness to get anything wrong."

I laughed.

"And the other possibility?" Bobby asked.

"The killer came up along the house under the windows where Ida and Jordan couldn't see him and took LaMarcus back that same way. LaMarcus could've been even closer to the house than they realized."

"But he would've seen him approaching," Bobby said. "Why didn't he scream? Say something?"

"Because it was somebody he knew and trusted."

"Like the dad," he said.

"Or the friend," I said. "Maybe like the boy we just borrowed to re-create it, he thought it was a game."

Chapter Nineteen

"Williams always dumped his victims' bodies far from where he picked 'em up," Bobby was saying.

We had walked through the wooded area on the back side of Ida's property and were now on the paved road of Flat Shoals Estates, the subdivision behind it, slanting down a hill to an empty cul-de-sac and another wooded area beyond.

Unlike the flat sand and dark dirt Florida terrain I was accustomed to, Georgia was all red slopes and orange slants of clay hills.

"Now just remember," Bobby said, "none of these houses were here."

Each structure was built at the end of an unnecessary curved driveway on an incline rising from the road. Three slight variations and sizes of the same brick front, vinyl siding surround, cookie-cutter version of mid-level starter homes.

"Be easy to go to the wrong home in a subdivision like this," I said.

"Happens a lot," he said. "We get calls all the time from people complaining about belligerent drunks breaking into their houses."

We reached the end of the street, stepped across the cement sidewalk and through a small wooded area in the midst of which was an enormous concrete drain pipe.

"This is where the body was found," he said. "Lying here inside this culvert like he was just taking a nap. Couldn't tell anything was wrong until we rolled him over and could see the small nylon rope around his neck."

"Still had his clothes on? Had he been messed with sexually?"

"All his clothes were on but his pants and underwear were down some and sort of wadded up. Like someone had pulled them down and then didn't get 'em back up just right."

"Had he been molested?" I asked. "Raped?"

He nodded.

"How long after he went missing was it before he was found?" I asked.

"Less than three hours."

"Who found him?"

"The partial retarded kid I told you about. Carlton Fields. Claims he was kicking a soccer ball in the cul-de-sac and it rolled in here. Came in after it and saw LaMarcus. Couldn't wake him up. Went and told his parents."

"I see why you suspected him," I said.

"Do far more after today," he said.

We stood there taking it all in for a moment, neither of us saying anything.

"See what I mean about this not fitting Williams's pattern? Body dumped so close to where he was snatched. And there are other, even more compelling reasons for it not being Williams."

"You said body being dumped—he wasn't killed here?"

He smiled. "You're pretty sharp for somebody studying for the priesthood."

I wasn't sure if he was kidding or didn't know I wasn't, but decided he probably didn't care and it certainly didn't matter.

"Wanted to show you this first," he said. "'Cause it's the

order we saw it in. Now I'll show you were he was killed."

"He was killed here," Bobby said.

We were back behind the daycare, in the wooded border on the right side of the property where he had run from when he came out to reenact the snatching of LaMarcus.

"So he was killed right after he was taken, not far from the spot where he was taken," I said. "Somethin' Williams never did that we know of."

"There was a small clearing inside here where he used to play," he said. "Sort of like a fort or hideout. Wasn't much. Just a little patch of clay where he'd play with Tonka trucks and matchbox cars surrounded by the bushes. Only a few feet wide."

"And Carlton?" I said. "Did he know about it? Play in it with him?"

"Probably. Never confirmed that. Did I let a kid get away with murder?"

"So why'd the killer move the body after he killed him here?" I said. "Why not just leave him here?"

"Why'd he *come back* and move him?" Bobby said. "The body laid here for a while before it was moved to the drainage ditch. So either the killer stayed here with him or left him and came back and moved him."

"You're right," I said. "Not much about this argues for it being part of the other pattern killings."

"And I haven't even gotten to the biggest reason we ruled Williams out," he said.

"Which is?"

"Remember I said we found a rope around his neck? There were some other marks too, indicating he was strangled, but . . . all of them happened post-mortem. Like the killer was trying to make it look like the others."

"So how'd he die?"

"What did I tell you it looked like he was doing when we found him in the drain pipe?"

"Sleeping."

"Cause of death was listed as undetermined for a long time," he said. "Wasn't until toxicology came back that we knew. He was put to sleep. The killer gave him something. He fell asleep. And never woke up."

Chapter Twenty

"Should my boy have been on the list?" Ida asked.

I shook my head. "I honestly don't think so."

Tears crested her eyes and trickled down her cheeks.

We were alone in the daycare center, seated in two rocking chairs on the reading rug, Jordan and the other teachers outside watching the children play in the late-afternoon sun-dappled yard.

"Serial killers create a series, follow a particular pattern," I said. "Ritual killers observe certain rituals. If they deviate, it's out of necessity not choice."

She nodded, wiping her cheeks and eyes.

"It's possible Wayne Williams killed LaMarcus," I said. "It looks like he was in the area that day, but I don't think he did. I really don't. I think whether Wayne Williams is innocent or guilty of the pattern cases on and off the list is irrelevant to what happened to LaMarcus. Someone else killed LaMarcus, someone still out there."

Her frown and the shake of her head seemed to communicate resignation more than anything else.

"Are you . . ." I began. "Were you hoping . . . for . . ."

"Always thought if I could get 'im on the list or convince people he suppose to be . . . I might find out one day what really happened. Nobody gonna do anything now . . . not if he not one of the . . . not part of the . . ."

"I don't think anybody's investigating any of the killings," I said. "On or off the list."

"You are."

I nodded. "I am."

"But if my son wasn't killed by the Atlanta Child Murderer, doesn't that mean you not gonna investigate what happened to him?"

"Just the opposite," I said.

She looked confused.

"If you'll let me and you're willin' to help me," I said, "I'd like to just focus on finding out what happened to LaMarcus."

"*Let you*?" she said, her face brightening. "*Willin'*? Boy, don't be silly. I'd be mighty . . . Thank you. Jesus. Thank you."

"Chances are I won't be able to turn up anything the police haven't," I said. "I don't have the access, expertise, or resources they do. All I can do is look at it with new eyes. Bring a fresh perspective. I can focus on it in a way they can't—or couldn't. Not that they're doing anything on it at the moment. That's why I'm letting go of Wayne Williams and the other cases for now. LaMarcus will get all of everything I have to give. And I won't stop. Not until I find the killer or die before I do."

"Thank you," Jordan said. "I can't tell you what it means to us."

"You're welcome," I said.

By the time I had reached my car she had caught up with me.

"I hope I can help bring some closure," I said. "Seems to me you could really use something good in your life."

She looked down but I caught sight of a smile twitching at the corners of her mouth.

"What is it?" I asked.

She shook her head.

"Tell me."

"Was just a random thought."

"I want to hear it."

"I . . . I just had the thought that *you're* the something good that's come into my life. You are, aren't you?"

"If I'm not," I said with a smile, "I'll do until something good comes along."

"Are you as good as you seem?" she asked.

I thought about it for a moment. "I am what I seem. I'm not attempting to seem something other than what I am, but we're all better and worse than what we appear to be."

"I guess we are," she said.

We were centered between two sounds. On the one side, the ruckus, rowdy, joyful noises of children playing filled my left ear and her right. On the other, the whoosh and whir of traffic zipping by in both directions on Flat Shoals Road.

"Larry's not as bad as he seems," she said. "I know most people only see one side of him, but there's another, better . . ."

I didn't respond.

She looked down again, this time without the sweet smile.

"I meant that most of us are capable of more and less selfishness than we seem," I said, "that we can be more altruistic and assholey depending. Bullying, abuse, addiction, mental illness, sociopathic behavior all fall far outside of that."

"Assholey?" she said with a smile.

"I study a lot of psychology."

Chapter Twenty-one

That night, after basketball and fish sticks with Martin, a little reading in a homicide investigation techniques textbook Frank Morgan had let me borrow, and catching up on a couple of chapters in my theology book, I took LaDonna Paulk out on a date.

The daughter of Don and Clariece, LaDonna was a central part of the family-run church, singing on Sundays and taking some classes with the rest of us during the week at EPI. Considered Chapel Hill royalty, she was a beautiful dark-eyed girl of nineteen or twenty with short black hair and a stable, settled maturity about her I found refreshing.

I wasn't taking her out in an attempt to get my mind off the unavailable Jordan Moore, but I could think of worse unintended consequences.

Told by the rest of the guys in the dorm that I had to take her somewhere nice, I got a recommendation from Randy Renfroe, the college's director of student affairs and the person who seemed to know more about Atlanta than anyone I had encountered, scrounged up all the money I could find, and took her to a place downtown I couldn't afford.

After she ordered, I ordered a salad and water, lying about my stomach bothering me, but could tell she wasn't buying it.

We talked for a while about Atlanta and the college and my transition, before our conversation turned to the church and religion.

"I really appreciate your approach," I said.

"My *approach*?"

"Fully committed but levelheaded," I said. "Like your dad. There's so much hysteria and bishop worship."

She smiled. "Guess it's inevitable."

I shrugged.

"You don't think so?"

"You're right. A certain amount is, but . . ."

"But what?"

"Probably shouldn't be saying this to the bishop's niece, but . . ."

"You can say anything," she said.

And I felt like I could. She was easy to talk to and, like so many people in her family and in the church, open and nonjudgmental.

"It's not exactly discouraged," I said.

She nodded.

Our food came and she immediately halved hers and insisted on sharing it with me.

"Thank you," I said.

"We didn't have to come here," she said.

"You kiddin'? I love this place."

"Close your eyes," she said.

I did.

"What's the name of the restaurant?"

Unable to come up with it I began to laugh.

After we finished our overpriced meal and were leaving, I realized how close we were to the hospital.

"Would you mind . . ." I began. "I hate to ask, but . . ."

"What?" she said. "Just say it. But just know I'm not puttin' out on the first date after only half a meal."

I laughed a long time at that, nodding appreciatively at her, catching the mischievous glint in her eye.

"Would you mind if we ran by Grady for a few minutes? Sorry, but there's someone I really need to see and I'm not sure if—"

"Of course," she said. "It's fine."

"You sure?"

"Positive."

While she graciously waited in the lobby, I went up to see Roger Lawson, a vibrant, young, talented filmmaker—at least that was what he used to be. Now he was a gaunt, weak, weary man, unable to lift his limbs without pain.

When I walked into his room, I was struck, as I always was, by the smell. It was the smell of decay, of defecation and disinfectant, of death and the process of dying.

Roger was dying of a new disease, a disease seemingly so selective it was only targeting gay men. I had been warned. I was taking my life in my hands. There was uncertainty as to how the death sentence was passed from person to person, and for all that was known I could be getting it right now just by breathing the same air as Roger.

As was often the case, he was asleep when I came into the room.

I stood there quietly for a while, a silent witness to his suffering.

He had been abandoned by his family and friends. His boyfriend and one of their best friends had already died from the same disease earlier in the year.

"John," he whispered.

"Hey," I said, stepping closer and taking his hand.

I resisted the impulse to ask how he was feeling or doing or to make smalltalk of any kind. I was here to listen, to be near, to be present.

"A . . . preacher came by . . . today," he said. "Think . . . it was . . . today."

His voice was weak and airy, and came out in small, halted, breathy bursts.

"Baptist or Pentecostal . . . I . . . think. Should've seen . . . him. Put . . . on . . . a . . . hazmat suit to come . . . in and tell . . . me . . . I was an abomination . . . and going . . . to hell."

I shook my head. "I'm so sorry. Wonder why they let him in?"

"Some of the doctors . . . and . . . nurses agree with . . . him."

"Guess religious assholes don't have a corner on the market on stupid."

His smile looked more like a grimace but his eyes showed the intent of the expression.

"You . . . really don't think I'm . . . going to hell?" he asked. "Sorry I ask you every time."

"If God's love is conditional, if she loves you less than I do and capriciously and vindictively flings people into hell, would you even want to go to heaven?"

"I . . . don't want . . . to go to . . . hell."

I realized how theoretical and unhelpful my question had been. There was nothing comforting or reassuring about it. It was too abstract, too academic, and I felt bad, felt as if I was failing him.

"You won't."

I genuinely and sincerely believed he wouldn't. But that's all it was—belief. It occurred to me that the preacher telling him he was going to hell and me telling him he wasn't weren't nearly as different as we seemed. We were men of conviction, of faith, of belief, and I found it deeply disturbing that we differed not in kind but type.

"I'm so scared," he said.

"I know. I'm sorry."

"I want my mama to love me again."

And more than anything in the world at that moment that's what I wanted too.

"I appreciate your approach," LaDonna said when we were back in the car, flying down I-20 toward Decatur.

I laughed. "Am I being mocked?"

"Only a little. Just in the *way* I said it."

I shook my head.

"I mean it though," she said.

"Okay," I said.

"No, I really do. I mean you're too earnest, too serious, and I think you hold yourself to a standard that's too . . ."

I laughed. "The whole appreciating my approach thing is not coming through."

"'Cause I haven't gotten to that part yet."

"If you'll recall, that was the *only* part when I said it to *you*."

"You're so . . . real," she said, ignoring me. "And . . . sincere. So compassionate . . . you seem so passionate about God, but you're one of the least religious people I've ever met. You're a . . . I was gonna say contradiction . . . but I'm not sure you are. It's just . . . you seem equally passionate about finding LaMarcus Williams's killer as you do ministering to Roger Lawson."

She's right, I thought. I am.

"Thank you," I said around the lump in my throat. "That's very . . . Thank you."

"You just might be really and truly unique, John Jordan," she said. "And how many people can you say that about."

"He who would be a man must be a nonconformist," I said.

"Or woman," she said.

"He who would be a woman is undoubtedly a nonconformist," I said.

Chapter Twenty-two

When I pulled up in front of my apartment in Trade Winds, Jordan Moore was waiting for me.

"Is everything okay?" I asked.

"Yeah. I just wanted to talk to you some more."

"What about Larry?" I said. "Is it okay for you to be here?"

"He's at work. Or with one of his women. And Trade Winds is the last place in the world he'd look for me."

"Home sweet home," I said, looking around.

"You look nice," she said. "Were you on a date? Do you have a girlfriend?"

I shook my head. "No girlfriend. Just a . . . casual date."

"With who?"

I told her.

"I know I have no right to be," she said, "but I'm jealous."

Touched by what she said, disarmed by her honesty and openness, moved by her vulnerability, I took her in my arms and hugged her for a very long time.

"Wow," she said. "Didn't realize just how much I needed to be . . . I can't remember the last time I was hugged. And don't think I've ever been hugged like that."

As she spoke, I realized how much I needed it too, how

much touch, warmth, contact, connection was missing from my life.

I was far from home, in a city not my own, surrounded by strangers and acquaintances.

I tried to remember the last time I had been hugged. Not the sideways, chest bump, double back tap of bros or the lean back, breast-avoiding, quick motherly kind in church, but a real, tight, intimate embrace where something like love and humanity passes between the huggers.

The last hug like that I had received and given was with Anna and it had been months before.

"Can we go somewhere and talk?" she asked.

"How about those swings over there," I said, nodding over between the tattered tennis courts and the basketball court Martin and I played on.

"Is it safe?"

"I seriously doubt it," I said.

"Okay."

We walked across the parking lot, up the small slope, through the damp grass, and sat in swings like I hadn't been in since childhood.

Facing each other, we both instinctively reached up and wrapped our hands around the chains.

"This is nice," she said.

"Luxury apartments come with a lot of perks," I said.

For a long moment we just moved back and forth a bit, enjoying the night, sounds of the unseen city all around us receding even further into the distance.

"It's not my fault he was taken, is it?" she said.

"No, it's not," I said. "And wouldn't've been even if you had been looking down and there was time for someone to run in and grab him."

"I could never figure what I had done wrong but I've lived with such . . . with so much guilt."

"It wasn't your fault."

She nodded. "Thanks to you, I know that now."

"Did anything out of the ordinary happen?" I asked. "Were you two pulled away to do anything for any length of time? Any emergencies? Anyone come to the door? Anything?"

She shook her head. "We never looked away for more than a few seconds at a time. And between the two of us maybe we didn't even do that. Mom got a phone call. I spilled my drink. We each went to the bathroom at different times, but when one of us wasn't looking—for whatever reason—the other one was. When Mom went to the bathroom I actually stopped wrapping, got up from the table, walked over to the window, and watched him from there the entire time. Even opened the window and talked to him through it."

I thought about it.

"We knew what was going on. It was in the newspapers every day, on the TV every night. That's the unbelievable part about it. I watched with all my might, really took it seriously, but no one watched him like Mom. No mother ever watched her son any closer than she did. No one. So whatever happened had to have happened when I was watching. Not her. It can't be her. Has to be me. I did something. Missed something. Have forgotten something."

"I don't think you did," I said.

She didn't respond and we were quiet a while.

"Was LaMarcus's dad involved with him? Did he ever come around?"

Her eyes narrowed. "I can only remember seeing him a couple of times. Stands out because it always involved conflict. You think he—"

"Just considering all possibilities."

"You'll have to ask Mom about him. I can't really remember much of anything about him."

I nodded.

"Tell me about LaMarcus's little fort in the bushes."

"I didn't even know it existed until he . . . until after he . . . I didn't realize it at the time, but I can see now that I was too wrapped up in my own little world. There was a lot I didn't know about LaMarcus, a lot I didn't appreciate. I was too much of a typical self-centered teenager. Something else I've felt guilty for since . . . all this time."

"Ida told me you were very good to him, like a second mom. Nothing about what she said sounded like a typical teenager."

"You're so . . ." she began. "Thank you. You're . . . you always respond with kindness. It's very rare."

"It's not all that rare," I said. "I think the company you've been keeping has caused you to forget that."

She nodded. "That's probably true."

"Can I ask you something? Can you tell me why you're with someone like Larry?"

"I . . . I'm not sure I can answer that. I'm not sure I know fully. I know it's not just one reason. Maybe this hasn't happened to you, maybe it never will, but there are times . . . Sometimes in life you wind up in a position, a place, a prison cell and you honestly have no idea how you got into it and you have no idea how to get out of it."

"Could it be . . . Is it possible . . ."

"What? " she said. "Just say it. It's okay. Just be honest."

"The way he treats you . . . the bullying, the abuse, the other women . . . You've mentioned how guilty you feel, how you blamed yourself for LaMarcus getting taken, for . . . for not knowing where his hideout was, for being what you called self-centered . . ."

"Yeah?"

"Is it possible you're punishing yourself?"

She started to say something but instead burst into tears. She cried for a while.

I waited.

Eventually, she nodded. "I've never thought of it that

way. No one's ever . . . I've just always thought I deserved any bad thing that happens. He hit me when I was pregnant the first time. I lost the baby. The second time . . . nothing he did to me ended the pregnancy, but he did enough so when the baby was born she had a lot of health issues. She was sickly all of her short life and then she died and I . . . I thought . . . you let your brother get snatched by a serial killer. No way God's gonna let you have a baby. No way. This is your fault. You did this. You deserve this. When I found out I couldn't have kids again . . . I thought . . . you deserve that too."

"But you didn't," I said. "You don't deserve bad things. You aren't being punished. You're not . . . You're punishing yourself."

"I've never seen it before, but you're . . . You wanna hear somethin' truly twisted? Part of the reason I've stayed with . . . Larry . . . part of what I kept thinkin' was . . . he lost a child too. I kept thinkin' we're the only two people on the planet who lost that child. We share somethin' no one else in the world does. And I can't really blame him when I'm the reason it happened. I'm the one being punished."

"What was her name?" I asked.

"Savannah," she said. "My little Savannah Grace. Thanks for asking."

"Yon," Martin said. "Yon."

He was crossing the parking lot in pajamas and socks, waving his small hand.

Jordan wiped her eyes.

"I can go over there to meet him if you need—"

She shook her head. "It's fine. I'm fine. Thank you. You've helped me more in the short time I've known you than anyone has in six years."

"'Ey Yon," he said when he reached us. "'Ut 'oo 'oin'."

"Just talking to my friend. This is Jordan Moore. Jordan, this is Martin Fisher."

She extended her hand and they shook and spoke.

"It's nice to meet you, Martin Fisher," she said.

"What're you doin' up?" I asked.

"Where's your mom?" Jordan asked. "Why are you up so late?"

Martin looked confused, then looked at me and told me he was hungry.

"You're in luck," I said. "I've got the best dinner rolls I've ever had, from the most expensive restaurant I've ever eaten at, right over there in my car."

He looked almost as confused as before.

"Come on," I said.

We walked over to my car and I offered each of them a roll.

"Half one with me," Jordan said.

I did.

And we stood there in silence beside the car, each eating our rolls, each seeming to enjoy them equally.

"These *are* good," Jordan said. "Where'd they come from?"

I laughed. "I have no idea."

Chapter Twenty-three

"You heard from your dad?" Frank Morgan asked.

I shook my head.

"Sorry to hear that."

I nodded.

"You plan on going home anytime soon?"

I shook my head again. "Between school and work and this . . . I can't right now."

The *this* was the LaMarcus Williams case. We were at GBI headquarters to talk to the medical examiner who had worked on the case.

"You can go in now," the secretary said, smiling in a way that made me think she might find Frank attractive. Then again, she might just be a pleasant person.

Dr. Donald Douglas was an overweight, older grayish man with an overgrown gray mustache, large glasses, and a gray toupee that didn't move when the skin around and beneath it did.

"Thanks for doin' this, Don," Frank said.

"Not a problem. Not a problem at all."

"This is John Jordan, the young man I was tellin' you about."

We shook hands and all took a seat in the small, function-over-form office of hard, cold metal surfaces and wood veneer and leatherette furniture.

"This for some kind of school report or somethin'?" Douglas asked me.

Frank nodded. "It is. This young man has a bright future in law enforcement and I'm trying to encourage him, give him all the help I can get, expose him to experts such as yourself."

I smiled and nodded, trying to disguise my surprise.

"And you wanted to talk about the LaMarcus Williams case?"

"Yes, sir."

He opened a file folder on his desk and began to glance through it, his small hazel eyes blinking behind his big, thick glasses.

"All right. Very well. Fire away."

"Okay," I said. "Can we start with what actually killed him?"

"We can—and it wasn't the little rope around his neck or any of the external marks on his body. We found high levels of chloral hydrate in his system."

"Of what?"

"Chloral hydrate. It's an organic compound, a colorless solid soluble in water. It's a sedative and hypnotic that's been used as a sleep-aid for people suffering from insomnia, but it's now mainly used as an adjunct to anesthesia to help sedate people, especially children, undergoing medical and dental procedures."

So that's how he was put to sleep.

"I'm not sure how much detail you want me to go into, but . . . it's derived from chloral by the addition of one equivalent of water and was discovered through the chlorination of ethanol by Justus von Liebig in 1832. Its sedative properties weren't published until 1869. Soon its use was widespread—even recreationally."

I nodded, encouraging him to continue.

"You've heard of a Mickey, right? A Mickey Finn. It's a solution of chloral hydrate in alcohol. They call 'em knockout drops. It's potent stuff. Truth is, we don't even completely understand how it works. It's believed that a chemical produced by chloral hydrate called trichloroethanol causes a mild depressive effect on the brain. But like I said, we don't know. It's been used in date rape and both accidental and intentional death."

Since I was supposed to be a student working on a school project, I wished I had a composition book to take notes in.

"You remember Jonestown? Their Kool-Aid had chloral hydrate in it. It was in Marilyn Monroe's system at her death. It was given to Mary Todd Lincoln for her sleep problems. Nietzsche used it for years. Some say it contributed to his nervous breakdown and insanity."

Hearing the name Marilyn Monroe brought a deep, dull ache I had to the surface and transformed it into a sharp pain, making me realize just how much I missed Merrill. And not just Merrill, but his mom. And not just them but home and family and friends and familiarity and, of course and always, Anna.

"So LaMarcus was given an overdose of chloral hydrate and . . ."

He nodded. "It put him to sleep and he never woke up."

I wondered if the killer meant to use chloral hydrate to knock LaMarcus out so he could transport him easily, and accidentally gave him too much, unintentionally killing him or killing him sooner than he planned.

"It wouldn't take much," Douglas was saying. "Kid that small."

"So it could've been an accidental overdose?"

He shrugged. "Sure, I guess, but—"

Frank Morgan said, "Why give it to him if not to kill him?"

"To sedate and calm him," I said. "As part of the abduction."

He nodded, appearing to think about it.

I looked back at Douglas. "Was chloral hydrate found in any of the victims of the Atlanta Child Murders?"

"I . . . I don't know the answer to that. I don't think so, but I'm just not sure. I didn't work those."

"I'll double check," Frank said, "but I don't think so either."

"Does use of chloral hydrate indicate someone with some kind of medical background?"

He shrugged and shook his head. "No, not necessarily. It could, but just as likely not. It wouldn't be required."

"Where would the killer have gotten it?"

"Lots of possibilities, but most likely in a hospital or pharmacy."

"Which would point to a medical professional or someone with access to those places, right?"

"Maybe, but it could've just as easily have been someone with a prescription or someone who stole it from someone with a prescription."

"What kind of prescription? What would it have been prescribed for?"

"Maybe anxiety or nervousness. God knows there was enough of that going around at the time. But more than likely a sleep aid for the treatment of insomnia."

"Was he raped?" I asked.

Douglas looked at Frank. Frank nodded.

"There was trauma consistent with aggressive, violent penetration," Douglas said to me, "but the evidence indicates the assailant wore a condom. There were traces of latex and liquid lubricant but no seminal fluid was recovered in, on, or around the body. And . . . based on the fact that the skin was abraded but not bruised—there was no bruising—what was done . . . to the victim . . . occurred after death."

"A school project?" I asked.

Frank and I were standing outside GBI headquarters near his car, a boxy blue sedan that screamed cop—particularly when he was in it.

He smiled. "You're young and unofficial. And you look even younger than you are. He probably thought it was a junior high school project."

"So what'd you think about what he said?" I asked.

"Interesting. What you said about the killer intending to use the drug to incapacitate him for transport makes sense. Especially snatching him from his backyard."

"You'll check to see if any of the victims on the list—or off of it—were given chloral hydrate?"

He nodded.

"Were any of them raped after they were killed?"

He shook his head. "No. But I'll double check—especially those not on the list. You think it's still possible Wayne Williams killed LaMarcus?"

I shrugged. "If there's evidence of chloral hydrate being used or post-mortem rape among other victims, we'll have to consider the possibility that the Atlanta Child Murderer killed LaMarcus—whether it's Williams or someone else."

Chapter Twenty-four

"This your first home-cooked meal since you been in Atlanta?" Ida asked.

"Why?" I said. "Am I eating it like it is?"

She and Jordan laughed.

The three of us were around the dinner table at Ida's. Before us, country-fried steak in white pepper gravy, mashed potatoes, turnip greens, and cornbread.

I was extremely hungry. It was extremely good. Evidently, I was eating energetically.

"Sorry, but it's so good my manners just flew right out the door."

"I like to see a hungry man eat," Ida said.

"And you haven't lost your manners," Jordan said. "You're just . . . sort of attacking the food."

"To answer your question, the Paulks have fed me several times."

Jordan's eyebrows arched above wide, questioning eyes and a cute, twisted mouth. "Oh have they? Any Paulk in particular?"

Ignoring her, I said to Ida, "Clariece is a very good cook too."

"Don't see how she do all she do," Ida said.

"Me either."

"Who?" Jordan said.

"Girl, what you goin' on about?" Ida asked.

Jordan smiled and winked at me.

I smiled back and mouthed, It was just one casual date.

Ida's small home was simple and unassuming, clean and uncluttered, warm and welcoming. Its walls and surfaces were filled with photographs of LaMarcus and what were obviously gifts from the children she had cared for over the years—Precious Moments porcelain figurines and other child-centered mementos. Joining them were LaMarcus's framed school certificates, field day ribbons, report cards, and art projects. Mixed in among them were pictures of Jordan, including a heartbreaking mother and child portrait of her holding the tiny Savannah Grace in her own small hands, but none of Larry—not even in those from her wedding day.

Underneath it all, there was an essential sadness, not unlike the one beneath everything else the two women were. It was as if both family and home were host to a foreign entity so deeply embedded it was now part of the structural DNA.

"You should've brought Martin," Jordan said. "Mom, John has the most adorable neighbor. He's—how old is he?"

"Twelve."

"He's twelve and they play basketball together and John feeds him and he just adores John."

"I'd say he not the only one," Ida said.

"Tell Mom what he said."

I shook my head. "I can't."

"It's the sweetest thing ever."

"You're embarrassin' him, child."

Jordan seemed more relaxed, less nervous, more happy, less hopeless than I had seen her before. Though in general she seemed to be improving in nearly every way over the past several weeks.

Larry was at work. He knew Jordan was having dinner

with her mom. As far as I knew, he didn't know I was joining them.

Looking away from them a moment, I glanced around the room again, this time spotting something in the far corner I hadn't noticed before. Partially wrapped Christmas presents. I knew instantly they were what these two ladies were working on when LaMarcus went missing. A Star Wars lunchbox and Star Trek Communicators were visible, which meant beneath the bows and wrapping paper the other packages must have held a Guess Who game, a GI Joe, a Rubik's Cube, a train set, and records. Some of the very gifts I was given when I was his age.

"Some of the guys in the dorm are very religious in an old-school way," Jordan said. "And they were talkin' to Martin—that's his name, Martin Fisher—about Jesus, tellin' him about how much good Jesus did, how he fed the hungry and helped people and taught love. And they asked him if he knew Jesus and he said yes—John. Isn't that the sweetest thing you've ever heard?"

Ida reached over and patted my hand.

"He's so small, and kind of frail and vulnerable," Jordan was saying. "Reminds me of LaMarcus in so many ways."

Ida nodded but seemed unable to speak, her eyes misting, her lips twitching. Eventually, she said, "I'm glad he's got you, John. I'd love for you to bring him to dinner sometime."

No one said anything else for a few moments and we each found our way back to our food, eating for a while in silence.

I thought about what an odd pairing Ida and Jordan were. They were so different—from their appearance to life experience—but what they shared, loss and need and tragedy, bound them in ways that were far more profound than their deepest differences.

"Making any headway on what happened to my LaMarcus?" Ida asked at last.

I nodded. "Some. Yes, ma'am."

"He's got some questions I couldn't answer," Jordan said.

"If now's not a good time . . ." I began.

"Now is fine," Ida said. "There is no good time."

I nodded, but still didn't say anything for a moment.

"Can we start with LaMarcus's dad?" I said eventually.

"Anthony is an immature, self-centered drug addict," she said. "He's no killer. And he wouldn't kill his own son. No way. I couldn't believe that in a million years."

"Okay," I said. "But addicts don't think straight. And their minds are often altered. And they do more damage by accident than most people do on purpose."

"We both know a thing or two about that," Jordan said.

Ida nodded. "We do. And you might be right. But . . . I just . . . can't believe he could kill his own . . . son . . . no matter what kind of state he was in."

The quality of her voice was changing. A tightness and slight tremor at its edges let me know she found the discussion upsetting.

"How often did he come around?" I asked.

"Not a lot. It'd sort of go in cycles. He'd come by a few times kind of close to each other, then we wouldn't see him for months."

"How comfortable was LaMarcus with him?"

"Okay . . . not super."

"Would LaMarcus have gone with him?"

"Depends when and where, but he wouldn't go far."

He didn't go far, I thought.

"Did he ever take him anywhere—with or without your permission?"

"A few times. When I was sure he was clean and sober. He took him to the mall. Playground. Ball game."

Her hands were beginning to shake a bit and the look of distress on her face was incrementally intensifying but I pressed forward.

"Ever take him or try to take him without your permission or pre-approval?"

She nodded. "One time. Said I was ruining his son, making him soft and girly. Said it took a man to raise a man and he was gonna take him and raise him up right."

I nodded and thought about it.

"You ready for some dessert?" Jordan asked. "We have bread pudding and ice cream."

"It sounds great but I'm so full, I—"

"You can take some home with you," Ida said.

"Thank you."

"You're not leaving now, are you?" Jordan said.

I shook my head. "I've got a few more questions," I said. "About Carlton Fields and the little hideout LaMarcus had."

"Can we . . . Would you mind if we wait on them?" Ida said. "I'm not sure I can handle any more at the moment. Talkin' about Anthony's stirred up some stuff, and I can only talk or think about what happened to LaMarcus a little at a time."

"Grief's a strange thing," Jordan said. "Sneaks up on you. You're fine one moment and not the next. You can handle things that should make you fall apart, and be reduced to a puddle by the smallest, seemingly most insignificant things."

I nodded.

Ida had gone to bed. Jordan and I were standing next to each other at the sink, washing and drying the dishes, our bodies touching at the side, our hands grazing as we passed plates and pots and glasses.

"She's so strong," Jordan said. "Can handle anything and then . . . she reaches her limit and has to shut down for a while."

"Is it the same for you?" I asked.

She hesitated, starting to say something, stopping, sighing, starting again. "Honestly, I stay more shutdown most of the time. I've had to. Or thought I did. To survive . . . to keep . . . functioning . . . on some level."

I reached down, plunging into the soapy dishwater, and took her tiny hand in mine and just held it.

And held it.

We stayed that way for a while, neither of us doing anything else but breathing.

"We're so damaged," she said. "*I'm* so damaged."

I didn't say anything. Just listened. Just held her hand.

That's it, I thought. That's what I'm called to do—help people damaged by violent crime, salve the suffering of the living while searching for some kind of justice for the dead. As both a minister and an investigator I'd be in a unique position to do both.

"But . . ." she said.

"Yeah?"

"Since you've come around . . ."

She left if out there a long moment. I waited.

"I've been less shutdown . . . and . . . sometimes . . . like now . . . I'm not shutdown at all."

That night I dreamt of Jordan.

Jordan standing in the backyard, a dark, depraved figure tearing out of the woods, racing toward her, snatching her, dragging her back by her sun-streaked hair into the thicket, me stuck in the house, unable to save her.

Little LaMarcus playing in the backyard, unaware of the simian creature careening toward him. Jordan dashing toward him, reaching, grasping, just missing.

Jordan holding a swaddled Savannah, kissing her cheek, smelling her skin, singing her the sweetest song I'd ever heard. Wayne Williams slithering up behind her, snatching Savannah from her, darting away. Jordan pleading with me to do something. Me unable to do anything.

In a car. Jordan in the passenger seat beside me. Savannah in a carseat in the back between LaMarcus on one side and Martin Fisher on the other. Family trip. Happiness. Jordan's bare feet on the dashboard, sun-kissed toes. Larry plowing out of a side road in a pickup, T-boning the car, sending it spinning down a deep ravine. Falling. Screaming. Crashing. Dismemberment. Death. Despair.

Chapter Twenty-five

"Dis some kinda school project?" Anthony Williams asked.

I nodded and smiled and made a mental note to try to age myself some. "How'd you know?"

"Why else a white boy be aksin'?"

It had taken several days, but I had finally tracked down LaMarcus's dad at a huge apartment complex off Memorial Drive where he was doing day labor for a turnkey company.

He was a narrow-framed, emaciated man with very dark skin, a permanently and deeply furrowed forehead, and a wide, flat nose, below which was a black-beginning-to-gray mustache in need of trimming.

Every cell of his moist skin shined with a greasy sheen.

The apartment he was working on was hot and had the lingering stench of rotting potatoes and urine, but it was no match for the odor emanating from Anthony Williams himself.

He was patching a much marred and pockmarked sheet-rock wall, the sweat pouring from him stinking of cheap booze, junk food, cigarettes, and drugs cut with something truly rancid.

The toxic body odor wafting off him stung my eyes and made me breathe very shallowly, but when he lifted his arm to reach the spots above his head it was unbearable.

"You know you's the first person to ever talk to me about what happened to my boy."

I shook my head.

"Po-lice aksed questions, but nobody else ever even mentioned it."

I wondered if anyone in his life even knew he had a son.

"I'm sorry to hear that," I said.

"Whatcha needs to know?"

Since he thought he was helping me with a school report I had to choose my first question carefully.

"Do you think Wayne Williams was responsible for what happened to your son?"

He shook his head. "That pudgy nigger ain't killed nobody. My kid or anybody else. He's framed. Ain't no killa of any kind. They just needed a fall guy."

"They?"

"Cops, mayor, business owners. White people what run this town. Didn't care if the real killer keep killin' little black boys. Long as they got everybody thinkin' it over."

"Do you have any idea who killed LaMarcus?"

"Oh, it was the same killer killed those other youngins. Just wasn't Wayne Williams."

"Any idea who it was?"

"Don't think we'll ever know. Powers that be don't want us to."

"When was the last time you saw LaMarcus before he died?"

"It had been a while. Crazy ex old lady never let me see him much."

"Why's that?"

"She crazy. I mean really bat shit bonkers, man. But mostly 'cause I broke her heart. She's gettin' back at me through the kid. Keepin' him from me. Hell, punished the kid more'n me. But . . . women . . . you know?"

I nodded as if I knew.

He shook his head. "The way she treated that boy . . .

like . . . he made of china or somethin'. Never let him do anythin', never let him have no fun. Made him weak and frail and . . . and then she go and marry a white man and try to make him white. No offense. Nothin' wrong with bein' white if you white but . . . notice she ain't tried to turn that white girl black."

"Did you try to stop her?" I asked. "Try to take him? Make a man out of him?"

He nodded. "Take a man to raise a man, I always say. Yeah. You get it. Yeah, I tried. Talked to him. Tried to get him to see, but he . . . she had . . . I tried to just, you know, take him with me without her knowin', but he was too far gone. Bitch had already ruined him."

"How'd you do it?" I asked. "With her watchin' him all the time the way she did, with her always smothering him . . . It'd be impossible."

"Wait 'til you're older, 'til you have kids. Nothin' you won't do for 'em, man. Nothin'."

"But how?" I said. "I don't see how it could be done."

"That's 'cause you not streetwise, young brother," he said.

"I guess so," I said. "It's just . . . I talked to her and I see what you're sayin' about how she is and the way she was over him . . . I've seen her old house, her yard . . . I just don't think it could be done. I can see why you didn't do it."

"You gots no imagination," he said. "There's nothin' to it. See the boy playin' in the back. Knock on the front door then run around to the back."

"But what if the girl goes to the door and his mama stays and keeps watchin' or his mama goes and the girl keeps watchin'?"

He shrugged.

"Duck under the windows where they can't see you," he said. "Call the boy over to you."

I nodded. "You're right," I said. "Wow. Ingenious."

He smiled.

"But what if she's got him so brainwashed he won't go?" I said. "What then? How could you save him from her like only a father can if he won't go?"

"You do anything to save your son," he said. "Give him somethin' if you have to."

"Like what?" I asked. "Something like chloral hydrate?"

"What?"

"Cough syrup."

He nodded and shrugged. "Yeah. Sure. Anything like that."

"Anything for your son," I said.

"Anything," he said, nodding even more defiantly. "Anything at all."

Chapter Twenty-six

I spent nearly all my free time over the next several days searching for a couple of subcontractors. When I wasn't in class or working or studying or visiting or spending time with Martin, I was looking for Raymond Pelton and Vincent Storr.

I had very little time, no resources, and really didn't know what I was doing. And it showed. For all my efforts, such as they were, I had exactly nothing.

I had nothing and I didn't know what else to do. Except ask for help.

I called Bobby Battle at home.

It was late to be calling, nearly ten, but I wasn't sure when I'd have another chance and the truth was I didn't want to wait.

"Hello?"

A female voice that didn't sound sleepy or irritated.

"May I speak with Bobby, please?"

"May I tell him who's calling?"

"John Jordan."

"One minute."

"John?" Bobby said.

"Sorry to call so late."

"It's early around here," he said. "What's up?"

"I was calling to see . . . I'm having a hard time finding

Pelton and Storr."

"Good."

"I was wondering if you could help me."

"With what?"

"Finding them."

"For what?"

He wasn't making this easy.

"So I can talk to them."

"Listen," he said. "Let me tell you something. The last thing you need to do is go anywhere near them. Understand?"

"No, I don't guess I do. I thought that was the whole idea."

"Look, talking about the case, even talking to the family, is one thing, but these are real bad men. There's no good outcome here. Best case . . . they tell you to go fuck yourself because you're a kid with no authority or jurisdiction of any kind. Worst case . . . they hurt or kill you."

"I'm not . . . I wasn't just gonna . . ."

"Tell you what, you let us handle guys like Pelton and Storr. Last thing you need to be going up against are career criminals like them. You had some good ideas at the crime scene. Morgan was right about you. You got a knack for certain aspects of detection, but theory is one thing, law enforcement is another."

I didn't say anything.

"I ain't tryin' to hurt your feelin's. I'm tryin' to save your life. You know how many cases I'm working right now? You know how many involve violent death? These people don't play. They will chew you up and spit you out. I got all these cases, but let me just tell you about one of them. This violent serial rapist motherfucker. He attacks this young girl, about your age, Brittany Ann. He beats her into submission and tries to rape her. When he can't get it up, he rapes her with a hammer. *A hammer.* But he doesn't kill her. That's a relief, right? He tells her she can go. When she stands to leave, he throws her down on her face this time and rapes her in the ass with the same hammer. What would a civilian say or do to a man like that? I'd like to know."

After hanging up the phone with Battle, I headed straight for the bottle of vodka I had hidden in the suitcase in my closet.

No orange or pineapple or cranberry juice. Just straight vodka from the bottle and keep it comin'.

I had been dismissed, belittled, treated like . . . what I was.

I was angry and frustrated, ready to burn something down—and mostly because he was right.

Who the hell was I? What could I do?

I drank myself to a point just shy of oblivion and then I passed out on top of my made bed fully clothed.

I slept. I dreamt.

Children. Sleeping. Dead.

They all looked so peaceful, so sweet in gentle, innocent repose, but they were all sleeping Shakespeare's sleep of death.

To die, to sleep—
No more; and by a sleep, to say we end
The Heart-ache, and the thousand Natural shocks
That Flesh is heir to? 'Tis a consummation
Devoutly to be wished. To die, to sleep,
To sleep, perchance to Dream; Aye, there's the rub,
For in that sleep of death, what dreams may come.

When I woke, I called Frank Morgan.

"Good morning, sunshine," he said.

I mumbled some incoherent response.

"Up all night praying?"

"I had a thought."

"Well, hold it. I checked the pattern cases' victims on and off the list as best I could and there's no indication any were drugged with that chloral hydrate stuff and none were raped after death."

"So LaMarcus doesn't fit in the ACM pattern," I said. "We expected that. But what if he's part of a different series? That's what I dreamt last night. A series of similar victims—children all appearing to be asleep but really dead, killed by the same guy who killed and raped LaMarcus."

"That'll take a lot longer to find out and I'll need to call in some favors for help searching the files, but I'll see what I can do."

"Thanks, Frank."

We were quiet a beat, a beat in which I could feel the dull ache in my head more acutely.

"I talked to Anthony Williams," I said.

"The victim's biological father? What'd he have to say? How'd you find him?"

I told him.

"You got him to say that?"

"I was thinking, what if it started as him just trying to get his son back so he could make a man out of him? Would explain the use of the drug and him leaving him in the bushes for a while."

"You're thinkin' the overdose was an accident?"

"Maybe. But it wouldn't explain why he dragged him into his hideout in the bushes."

"I don't follow."

"I mean that particular spot. How'd he know about it?"

"Maybe the kid told him. Maybe he watched for a while before he tried to snatch him. Maybe it was the only clearing back there."

"Maybe," I said, "but what none of it explains is the rape. It's one thing to try to snatch your kid and accidentally kill him, panic and move the body, maybe even stage it to look like something other than what it was, but to rape him . . ."

"Yeah," he said. "Would seem to rule out it being an accidental overdose or the dad being the doer . . ."

"Unless," I said, "someone else came along, found him dead, and raped him."

"Two crimes," he said, his voice, rising, "two criminals. A killer and a rapist. Could be. Could very well be."

Chapter Twenty-seven

After my morning classes, I drove down to Willie's German Bakery in the shopping center at the corner of Flat Shoals and Wesley Chapel, grabbed a bag full of eclairs and M&M iced cookies, and drove over to Safe Haven.

The dull ache in my head felt just bad enough to be mildly annoying, but occasionally it throbbed, the pressure pounding with my heartbeat, the pain shooting down my spinal cord.

"Well, look who it is," Ralph said. "Who could've predicted this? The man with too much time on his hands."

"You sure you're not happy to see me?" I said. "I brought you an eclair."

"I wouldn't say no to an eclair," he said, "but listen to what I have to say first and see if you still wanna give it to me."

"Okay."

He stepped outside the fence and away from the gate to speak to me.

"These poor ladies have been through enough," he said. "They don't need you to keep dredging up the most horrific nightmare they ever lived through . . . giving them false hope, raising their expectations . . . all for nothin'. It's never gonna be solved. Not ever. 'Specially by the likes of you. All *you're* doin' is wasting time and doin' harm to two people I care about. And why? 'Cause you're new in town and need somethin' to do, need some attention from a sweet mama and a pretty girl? Well, the cost is too high. And I'm not gonna let you keep doin' it. Understand?"

"I understand what you're sayin'," I said. "And I genuinely appreciate your concern. I do. Ida and Jordan deserve it. They do. But I'm not doin' what you're accusin' me of. It has nothing to do with me not having enough to do or wanting attention, and I wouldn't be doin' it if I didn't think I could help figure out who did it."

"Never happen," he said.

"And you think I'm wrong to even try?"

He nodded. "Because of what it'll do to them. This ain't no game or some movie or somethin'. This is people's lives. Good people. This isn't theory or book stuff. This is the real world where people are barely makin' it and you can do damage they can't come back from. And if you're just tryin' to sleep with Jordan, stop it. This ain't the way to go about it and you don't need to anyway. She's married and too old and too good for—"

"Who is?" Jordan asked as she walked up. "Who's too old and too good for who?"

"Ma'am?" Ralph asked.

"Who is?"

"I . . . I was just . . ."

"I went by Willie's," I said, holding up the bags. "Trade you a little sugar for a little info."

She turned her attention away from Ralph and onto me, smiling in the process.

"Sounds good. Ralph, we'll talk about this later. Give you time to remember what you meant."

"Yes, ma'am."

She turned and began walking away. I followed, pausing long enough to open the bag and extend it toward Ralph.

"Eclair?" I offered.

"Seriously?"

I nodded.

He started to reach for one but stopped. "You gonna snatch the bag back when I—"

"NO," I said. "Honest offer. Don't make the lady wait. Grab one. Hell, grab two."

He did.

"What was that about?" Jordan asked.

"Just him being protective over you and your mom."

"I don't understand."

"He doesn't approve of what I'm doing. Thinks I'm stirring things up. Wasting time. Raising false hopes. And he questions my motives. Particularly where you're concerned."

She smiled. "Sorry about that. I think he's always had a bit of a crush. And he is very protective over Mom and me and the kids and everything Safe Haven. Feels like it's his job to keep us all safe—and I guess it is . . . but he goes way beyond . . ."

"What's his story?"

"Been our neighbor for as long as I can remember. Lives right over there."

She turned and pointed behind us to the small red brick house on a hill beyond the many fences of Safe Haven.

"He was so helpful when LaMarcus went missing, calming us, searching the area, dealing with the police. After we found out LaMarcus was . . . gone . . . he helped me and Mom in every way imaginable. He was a cop at one time, but has worked security at South Dekalb mall for . . . well, since I can recall. That's what he was doing when Mom decided to open Safe Haven and offered him the job. He knew how important it was to her to make the safest place possible for children and he took a pay cut to take the job."

I opened the bag of cookies and offered it to her. We each took some and ate them as we looked out across the empty playground and Ralph kept looking at us.

"Damn you, Willie," she said, shaking her fist in the air in mock outrage. "Why do these cookies have to be so good?"

I laughed and we ate some more.

"I talked to Mom," she said. "Got some more info for you. Seems like that may be the best way for her. Just let me know what you need, and I'll ask her when I know it's an okay time and let her tell me in her own way and on her schedule."

"Thank you," I said. "So you don't think I'm wasting time or stirring up things and raising false hopes?"

She shook her head. "The thing Ralph and so many others don't understand is how much it stays stirred up. If you're wasting anybody's time it's your own, but I don't think you are and I appreciate everything you're doin'. Just the fact that you're interested, that you are—that *someone* is still doin' somethin' about it . . . not just filing it away as another unsolved murder of a black boy . . . It means more than you'll ever know."

I nodded, my heart filling, my spirits being buoyed again.

"I do hope Ralph was right about one thing at least," she said.

"Oh yeah? What's that?"

"I hope your motives in regards to me are not as pure as they appear."

I smiled. "I wasn't aware they appeared pure at all, but if they do . . . just remember . . . things aren't often what they appear to be."

"Thank you for saying so," she said. "It's sweet."

We fell silent a moment, munching on the small cookies, enjoying each other's company, taking in the magnificent midmorning sun and the way the fall foliage basked beneath it.

"Mom said that LaMarcus worked very hard to keep his little hideout a secret. And he must've done a good job because I didn't know about it. But as I said, I was a self-involved teenager. Mom knew and kept an eye on him when he was in it—but he didn't know she knew about it. After the killings started, he wasn't allowed in it because she didn't want him out of her sight."

"That was something I meant to ask you before," I said. "Why didn't y'all look in there first? When he first went missing, why not look in his hideout before y'all did anything else?"

"We thought we did, that someone did. I was just finding out about it. The whole thing was . . . everything was pandemonium. We were all just rushing around like crazy. I thought Mom checked it. She thought I did. It was . . . It never got checked. At least not in time."

I nodded.

"Before that," she continued, "he used to play in it a good bit. The only other person she knows for sure who knew about it and played in it with him was Carlton."

"Carlton Fields, the neighbor boy who found . . . the . . . LaMarcus?"

She nodded.

"He not only knew where it was but played in it with LaMarcus?"

"Uh huh, but you can't suspect him. He's the sweetest boy in the world, a true innocent. He functions at a pretty low level, but he's guileless."

"I need to talk to him."

"Well, it won't be hard to do," she said. "His mom's back in school and is always looking for someone to keep him on Tuesday and Thursday nights."

Chapter Twenty-eight

After leaving Safe Haven, I went back to EPI to find a phone.

Pam Palmer, the college's registrar, was just leaving for lunch and said I was welcome to the use of hers and the privacy her office afforded.

I called Bobby Battle again. This time at the station.

"Last night's conversation went so well," I said, "figured I'd call you again."

"Sorry if I was discouraging," he said, "but I'm a straight shooter and I'm just lookin' out for you. Shit we deal with is no joke."

"I know," I said, just to be saying something.

"Got a lot goin' on," he said. "What can I do for you."

"Ralph Alderman," I said.

"What about him?"

"Why'd he leave the force to become a mall cop?"

"He's a fuckup. Always was. Didn't fuck up quite bad enough to become captain but just bad enough so that he had to go."

"What'd he do?"

"Wasn't just one thing. It was a lot of shit over a long period of time. Take your pick. Some personal, some professional, some procedural, some just being a fat ass with an annoying personality."

"Did you look at him for LaMarcus Williams?"

"No. Why?"

"Not even briefly to exclude him?"

"No," he said. "Hell, he helped us. Functioned like one of the team. Why?"

"Just askin'. Tryin' to be thorough."

"Come on," he said. "What'd he do to make you suspect him?"

"Nothin'. Just—"

"Probably should've looked at him," he said. "Don't bust my balls about it. I would if the investigation was now. I've learned a thing or two since then."

"Can we look at him now?"

"*We?*"

I didn't say anything, just waited.

"I'll dig around and see what I can find out, but chances are he's got nothin' to do with it."

"But if there's even a slim chance . . ."

"I said I'd look into it. Take the win. Quit tightening the noose around my neck, and be grateful."

"I am. Thanks. What about a current cop? Larry Moore?"

"You don't think he had anything to do with it, do you? Larry's got no class and a bad temper but he's no child killer."

"No, I don't," I said. "Just asking about him. He's married to the victim's sister."

"Then more's the pity for her," he said. "Guy's a major asshole. But he's a decent enough cop. I think. He ain't gonna break a sweat bringin' in a bad guy, but he ain't crooked or anything. Far as I can tell. Okay, fun chattin' with you, but I've got to run."

After I hung up with Battle, I walked into the empty chapel and prayed and meditated for a while, then downstairs to the janitor's closet and the cleaning cart awaiting me there.

For the next few hours I vacuumed and dusted the classrooms, scrubbed and mopped the bathrooms, vodka pouring out of my pores, the pounding in my head increasing, as I thought about how and why LaMarcus Williams died and who might have done it, about Wayne Williams and if he was guilty or not, who would and would not make my list, were I to make one, about the nature of justice and the way of the world, about Jordan Moore and Ida Williams and the suffering only a mother can know, about my own mother and father and my home and—

"So why *do* the innocent suffer?"

I turned to see Jordan standing in the doorway.

"Hey. What're you doing here? Is everything okay?"

She nodded toward the chalkboard in the front of the classroom. On it was written *Why do the innocent suffer?*

The class belonged to Pastor Jim Oborne, one of the most popular and academically rigorous of the EPI instructors. It was the single remaining remnant of an inspiring and invigorating lecture and discussion about the nature of suffering.

"I had a short break so I walked down to have you tell me why the innocent suffer, why the wicked are rewarded, why the good are punished."

I laughed.

"Well, I came to see you, but I *would* like to know."

"Wouldn't we all," I said.

"Seriously," she said. "Tell me."

"I don't know," I said. "There are a lot of theories, but . . ."

"None you buy?"

I shrugged. "Only one," I said, "but the truth is asking why is mostly a waste of time. Knowing the why of suffering won't change it, won't change anything. Dealing with suffering, sitting with the suffering, alleviating suffering, when and where we can . . . that's far more . . . useful."

She nodded, narrowing her eyes, pursing her lips—agreeing but still considering it too. "Makes sense. A lot actually. But . . ."

What could I possibly tell this woman about suffering?

"I have to know the one thing," she said.

"What's that?"

"The one theory you buy about suffering."

"Freedom," I said. "I don't just mean human beings. I mean the entire universe. If freedom is built into everything . . . it allows for the possibility of everything—including suffering. Including the suffering of the innocent. Freedom means there's order but there's also chaos. There's love but there's also indifference. There's altruism but there's also selfishness. There's unspeakable joy but there's also unimaginable horror. I don't know. That's just another bullshit theory like all the others. Means nothin' to nobody in the face of true suffering."

"So true," she said.

"What? That I'm full of bullshit?"

"NO, I meant—"

"I know what you meant," I said.

"Spend less time wondering why we suffer and more time dealing with suffering," she said.

I nodded. "Exactly. More time helping ease the suffering of others."

"Well, you're certainly doing that, John Jordan," she said. "You're certainly doing that."

Chapter Twenty-nine

I finally found Vincent Storr a few days later.

He was working on remodeling an old farmhouse on Flakes Mill Road near Ellenwood, ripping out pinewood paneling and replacing it with sheetrock.

Except for the traffic on Flakes Mill, the area was quiet and had a rural feel—scattered houses on wooded lots, some of which were fenced with livestock in them.

Before I moved up here, I would never have imagined such an area in Metro Atlanta so close to downtown.

I parked on a white gravel driveway beneath an enormous oak tree that dappled the yard and part of the house with mid-morning sunlight, and walked toward a worker cutting sheetrock board on the front porch, the gravel crunching beneath my shoes as I did.

When I asked for Storr, he said, "What're you? An illegitimate child who's just tracked him down?"

"Something like that," I said.

"He's right inside," he said. "Go on in."

As I opened the door, he yelled, "VINCE. VINCE. SOMEONE HERE TO SEE YOU."

Storr was a tall, meager man with wispy, thinning black hair, deep, dark, sunken eyes, and the very heavy, very dark stubble of a five o'clock shadow at ten in the morning.

He wore white painter's pants, a loose white crew neck undershirt, and penny loafers—all of which, and every inch of him, was covered in white sheetrock dust.

He was holding a bucket of mud in one hand and a trowel in the other, eyeing his work on a seam where two boards joined together.

The beautiful white pine board paneling was still up on one end of the room and I admired it a moment before I said anything to him.

"Why would you pull down that and replace it with sheetrock?" I asked, shaking my head.

"Only one reason," he said, looking around and lowering his voice, "niggers."

I was taken aback by his blatant racism before a total stranger and the sad assumption associated with it, but I did my best not to let it show. I needed to see and hear from the real Vincent Storr, unadorned, unguarded, unsuspecting.

"I hope you're plannin' on takin' the wood with you."

"Take wood everywhere I go, if you know what I mean," he said. "But, nah, fuckin' boss is takin' it."

"Figures," I said, shaking my head.

"What can I do you for?" he asked.

"Lookin' for a painter," I said.

"Only do sheetrock."

"Think you've worked with him before. Raymond Pelton. I really like what he did on a house over off Flat Shoals Road."

He looked at me, narrowing his eyes suspiciously and studying me. "What house?"

"One in Flat Shoals Estates. Did you work with him on one over there?"

"Sheetrock crew is long gone by the time painters come in," he said. "Don't know no painter named Pelton."

"Oh, okay," I said.

"Why would you think I would?"

"Someone told me," I said.

"Someone told you, huh? Who?"

I could tell he wasn't buying it and I felt like an idiot. I should've prepared better, should've had a contingency plan in case the first one didn't work, but as it was there was nothing I could do but try to double down on the losing hand I was backing.

"Guy doin' some work over at the church I go to. Chapel Hill."

He nodded. "Guy got a name?"

"I'm sure he does, but I didn't get it. Do you know the subdivision I'm talkin' about? It's behind where that kid got killed."

He seemed to think about it for a long moment. "Oh, yeah, the little niglet. Now I remember. I did meet a painter on that job. Had to go back and patch a wall the flooring guy fucked up and I met him. Pelton. Bet I can find him. Just leave me your name, address, and phone number and I'll have him get in touch with you."

"Thanks."

"Here," he said, handing me a pen and a scrap of paper, both covered in a fine white powder.

The worker I had encountered on the porch brought in two pieces of sheetrock, set them down against the far wall, and walked out again without saying anything.

"They never caught whoever killed that kid," I said as I wrote down my info.

I tried to make the remark seem offhand, casual, idle, but that wasn't how it sounded to me.

It was hard to imagine doing a worse job at this. I felt slow and stupid. I had so much to learn—even more than I realized.

"Thought that soft, big fro nigger with the glasses did it. What was his name? Wayne Williams—same as the little boy who he killed then fucked."

The fact that LaMarcus had been raped had never been released to the public, and only a handful of tightlipped cops and the killer knew the rape came after the murder.

Something inside me began to buzz.

"You 'bout got that?" he said, nodding toward the paper. "I gotta get back to work."

I handed him the paper.

"John Jordan," he read. "Forty-three-thirty-six Pleasant Point Drive. Decatur."

I nodded.

And then I witnessed a transformation from something that had appeared to be a man into something that more closely resembled a monster.

"Now we know where you live," he said. "Ray and I will come pay you a little visit. We usually don't like 'em as old as you but we can make an exception. Bet your little pink pucker is still nice and tight. Is, ain't it?"

How could I be so stupid?

Everything about him had changed. He didn't even look like the same person any longer. He was even giving off a different odor, the smell of something feted and feral.

I didn't say anything, just stood there staring at him, my fists clinched at my sides.

Bobby Battle had been right about these men and about me. They were animals, cold, cruel, inhumane. I was ill-equipped, in over my head, and had just made a costly rookie mistake that could get me hurt or killed—just like Battle had said.

"Come in here talkin' 'bout somebody told you I might know Ray. Either you think my setting is stuck on stupid or yours is."

"It's clearly the latter," I said.

"Admitting it is the first step. So what's your story, stupid?"

"I'm an amateur—"

"That's obvious."

"Just tryin' to figure out what happened to LaMarcus Williams."

"Why?"

I shrugged. "Need to know."

"We all have needs," he said. "Some far more dangerous than others. Some'll cause you not to fit in, not to be able to live by society's bullshit rules. Others'll get you killed."

I had nothing for that so I kept my mouth shut.

"You too young to be a cop. Already said you's a amateur. You a friend of the family or just some random motherfucker with a death wish?"

"Tell you what," I said, trying to sound far more calm and unafraid than I felt, "I'm shy when it comes to talking about myself. Why don't we wait until you and Ray visit and I'll let my friends from the force tell you all about me. And if there's anything they don't know, Frank Morgan with GBI will. Here's his card in case you want to reach out to him directly. I'll make sure he's expecting to hear from you either way."

"I screwed up," I said.

There was a pause.

I wanted to call Frank, but knew it had to be Bobby Battle.

Swallow my medicine. Straight, no sugar.

"Let me guess," he said. "You tried to make a citizen's arrest and got your ass kicked."

"Worse."

He sighed heavily, his frustration and disapproval palpable even through the phone.

"Let me have it."

I did.

"Told you, didn't I?"

"You did. I'm sorry. I should've listened. I underestimated him and was unprepared and made a mess of it."

"Yes you did."

"But—"

"Make an excuse right now and I'll walk away, hang you out to dry. Let you deal with Pelton and Storr."

"He let it slip that he knew LaMarcus was raped."

"Doesn't take much to make that leap."

"After he was murdered."

"Oh."

He was quiet a moment.

"What'd you say to get him to say that?"

"Nothin'."

"You had to say somethin'."

"I said somethin' about how the killer had never been caught and he said he thought Wayne Williams did it and went on to say his last name was the same as the little boy who he killed then fucked."

"And you're sure it was just like that? He wasn't repeatin' or respondin' to somethin' you said, not inferring what happened from somethin' you let slip?"

"Positive."

"Well, then," he said. "You still fucked up, but maybe I won't let you get killed over it."

Chapter Thirty

"You remember LaMarcus, don't you, Carlton?" Jordan was saying.

She was holding up the last picture ever taken of her brother, one that was still on the roll of film inside Ida's camera when he was killed.

In it, he is skating at a friend's birthday party in Conyers, a large gold chain around his neck, a broad, sweet smile on his face.

Carlton nodded.

We were in the back corner of Safe Haven—me, Martin, Jordan, and Carlton—having waited until everyone else, including Ida, had gone home.

Jordan had told Carlton's mom it would be a little later than usual when she dropped him off tonight. Carlton's mom seemed grateful for the extra time.

Martin was with me because he wanted to be, had nowhere else to go, and I thought he might make Carlton feel safer. He sat at a table not too far from us, coloring with conviction.

"LaMarcus was a good boy," Carlton said. "LaMarcus was my friend."

Carlton had a big frame and a soft, fat belly emphasized by his too-tight, tucked in T-shirt, which was shoved deep into cheap, old, ill-fitting polyester pants cinched at the waste by a wide, brown, faux leather belt.

"He was," Jordan said. "He was a very good boy and he was a very good friend."

"LaMarcus died," he said. "LaMarcus is dead. He's in heaven with the angels."

I was letting Jordan ask the questions not only because of her rapport with Carlton and her quiet, kind, gentle ways, but because of how I had handled things with Vincent Storr.

"That's right," Jordan said. "LaMarcus, your good friend, is in heaven now."

"With the angels."

"With the angels, yes."

I had to keep reminding myself that Carlton was older than I was by a few years. Everything about him but his size was small, stunted, childlike.

"Do you remember what happened to him?" Jordan asked.

"LaMarcus wouldn't wake up. He went to sleep and wouldn't wake up."

"Did you try to wake him up?"

"I did. I did try to wake him up. *Wake up, LaMarcus. Wake up. Let's play some more.* But he wouldn't wake up."

More. He had said let's play some *more.*

"Had you been playing with LaMarcus before he went to sleep?"

Carlton nodded.

"Where? When?"

"LaMarcus played with Carlton. Hide. Count. Look. Ball. Carlton loves ball. Carlton and LaMarcus love basketball."

"'Ee 'oo," Martin said softly without looking up or missing a stroke with his crayon.

I smiled and thought about how much I enjoyed playing basketball with Martin.

"What did you and LaMarcus play the day he died, the day he wouldn't wake up?"

Carlton looked confused, as if the concept of time was too much for him, as if what his mind stored wasn't locked down and ordered, but rather tossed in and jumbled.

"LaMarcus played with Carlton. Nobody else. *Get outta here you fat retard. Go on. Get.* Just LaMarcus. Sweet, good boy LaMarcus."

Jordan swallowed hard and I caught the glint of gathering moisture in her eyes.

"LaMarcus told Carlton a secret," he said.

Jordan sat up, her head turning slightly, her expression rising.

"What did he tell you?" she asked.

"It's a secret."

"You can tell me," she said. "I'm Jordan, LaMarcus's sister. Remember?"

He shook his head. "*Can't tell anyone. No one. Promise me. I promise, LaMarcus.*"

"The thing is . . . after someone goes to sleep, after they die, you can tell their secret to their sister."

"You can?"

She nodded. "Yes. You can."

He looked over at me and then at Martin.

"We'll step outside a minute," I said. "Let you two talk."

"You color really well," I said to Martin when we got outside.

"'Ank 'oo, Yon."

With nowhere to go, we just wandered around a bit beneath the covered walkway.

It was a dark night, touched at the edges by a rim of pale moonlight. A cool breeze blew leaves about, their stiff edges scraping against the concrete of the walkway and the asphalt of the parking lot.

"Is Carl'on 'onna be o'a?"

I nodded. "He'll be fine, buddy. He's just helpin' us with something very—"

"The fuck you doin'?"

I turned to see Ralph Alderman rushing toward us.

He was out of his security uniform and looked odd, out of place in street clothes. He was wearing a navy-blue-and-white Nike jogging suit with only a wife beater and a gold chain beneath. Elephantine exercise clothes on such an enormously soft, fat man looked absurd and comical, as if he were a retired gangster.

"Waiting on Jordan," I said. "What about you? Out for a jog?"

"Where is she? What are y'all doin' here this late? Where's Miss Ida? Who is this?"

"Jordan's finishing up in the classroom. We're about to leave. Ida's at home. This is Martin Fisher, my best friend in Atlanta."

"Come on," he said. "I wanna hear it from Miss Jordan or I call the police. I'm sure they'd be happy to dispatch her husband."

We followed him to the classroom, my hand on Martin's shoulder.

"Everything's okay," I told Martin. "Nothin' to worry about."

He shrugged, seemingly not worried about anything.

When Ralph reached the door, he opened it and looked inside—and drew back as if he had seen something shocking.

I rushed around him to look inside, my heart pounding, my mind preparing for something horrible.

But everything was just as we had left it, Jordan and Carlton in the corner talking.

"Just be sure to lock up when you leave," Ralph said, quickly heading back down the walkway.

"What's wrong?" Jordan asked. "What was that about?"

She had walked over and was nearly to us.

I shook my head. "I'm not sure. He was all gung-ho to talk to you until he opened the door, and then he couldn't get out of here quickly enough."

"'Ome'in' 'ong wi' 'Arl'on," Martin said.

We looked back over to the corner where Carlton was.

He was rocking back and forth, his clenched fists up near his head shaking. "Carlton go home now. Time for Carlton to go home now. Take Carlton home."

We rushed over to him.

His pants, the chair, and the floor around him were wet where he had urinated on himself.

"It's okay," Jordan said. "It's no problem at all. I'll get you cleaned up in no time."

"No clean up. Go home. Carlton go home right now."

Chapter Thirty-one

"Carlton was seriously terrified of Ralph," Jordan said.

I nodded.

Martin and I had followed her to take Carlton home, waiting in the car down the way a bit while she had walked him in and gotten him situated. Then we had come to the Dairy Queen on Wesley Chapel for ice cream and were at the tables outside—Jordan and I sitting on top of one, our feet on the bench, licking our soft serve chocolate cones, Martin atop another finishing up his art project, his pencils and crayons spread out around him. Each time he traded one pencil, pen, or crayon for another, he took a bite of his banana split.

"I wonder why?" she said.

"Maybe he saw him kill LaMarcus."

"*Ralph*?" she asked, her voice rising in shock.

"Yeah."

We were talking quietly so Martin couldn't hear us, aided by his concentration and the traffic on both Wesley Chapel and I-20.

"No," she said. "There's no way. It can't be. It's got to be something else."

"Maybe," I said. "Maybe he reminds him of someone or maybe . . . Do he and Ralph have a history? Has anything happened at Safe Haven or—"

"No. Nothing. I don't think Carlton's ever been to Safe Haven before tonight. I just don't get it. I've never seen him like that."

"So you're saying he hasn't been around Ralph since LaMarcus was killed?"

She shrugged. "I don't know. I don't guess so. Not at Safe Haven anyway. But he would've had to have been back around the time it happened, at the funeral, visitation, in the neighborhood Carlton's family moved to. I . . . I'm just not sure. But it can't be Ralph. He's . . . He's around children every day."

"Exactly."

"But . . . to protect kids. He's there to . . . He takes his job of protecting the kids, of protecting all of us, so seriously. It can't be Ralph. He can't be . . . He wouldn't . . . He couldn't. Not Ralph."

"The more you say it, the more untrue it sounds."

"That's because the more I say it, the more I doubt it."

"Think about how hostile he's been toward us looking into what happened to LaMarcus, how threatened and defensive he's been. Maybe it isn't that he doesn't like me or has a thing for you. I've got to find out why he was fired from the force and we need to take a closer look at him."

"If he . . . if he killed LaMarcus and has been working for us all these years, pretending to care, pretending to protect . . ."

"I know."

This time when Martin put down his pencil, he took several bites of the banana and mixed the strawberry and chocolate ice cream together, his open mouth lingering over the plastic boat as he studied his work.

"Did he tell you LaMarcus's secret?" I asked.

She nodded as she finished the bite of cone she was working on, then said, "He did. Said LaMarcus told him he was going to live with his dad, that his dad was going to make a man out of him."

I thought about that, wondering when he had been told, why it stuck in his memory, and how it could fit with what had happened to LaMarcus.

Up near the street a white kid carrying an enormous boombox on his shoulder strolled by on the sidewalk in tight, black jeans tucked into black combat boots and a blue blazer customized with pins and buttons and patches. Rising out of shaved black hair, his spikey mohawk was white-blond. His ghetto-blaster was blasting a radio-recorded version of Run D.M.C.'s Walk this Way so distorted it was nearly unrecognizable.

"Could it be Anthony?" she asked.

I nodded.

"So not Ralph after all."

"It could be Ralph."

"But wouldn't his dad be more likely?"

"Could be both."

"*Both*?"

"Dad tries to drug him and take him away—to make a man out of him—but he gets the dose wrong and instead of calming him or putting him to sleep temporarily, kills him. He hides him in the bushes where he was just hiding before, then he flees. Ralph comes along, takes the body to the drainage pipe. Carlton sees him do it or sees him leaving after he did it and . . ."

"But why move LaMarcus to the drain pipe?" she asked.

She must not know about her brother being raped and I wasn't going to be the one to tell her. Not now. Not like this.

I shrugged. "It's just a theory."

"What're you gonna do?"

"Talk to Frank and Bobby."

She nodded.

We had both finished our cones and as our conversation came to a close, now found ourselves watching Martin as he alternated between his split and his drawing.

We sat there like that a long moment, our thighs touching, the sweet smell of her shampoo wafting over occasionally.

"I . . ." she began.

"Huh?"

"Nothin'. It was silly."

"Tell me. You can tell me. You can tell me anything. You could never be silly."

She looked at me with her sweet, kind eyes and her fresh, unadorned face, and smiled a beautiful but shy smile.

"I keep havin' this fantasy," she said.

"Oh yeah? Wonder if we're havin' the same one?"

"I know I shouldn't. Know it's silly and farfetched . . . but it's so . . . persistent. I guess it's more a picture in my head or a dream . . . I don't know."

"What is it?"

"It's us. Like this. Together. Married. Having adopted Martin. A family."

I nodded. "Sounds like a small sliver of heaven."

"So . . . you don't think . . . I'm . . . I don't know . . . you don't think it's wrong to even wish for?"

"It's lovely," I said. "And very similar to mine."

"Really?"

"Mine's the same as yours except in it Martin's in his room, in his bed sound asleep, and we're naked in ours in the way only lovers can be."

Chapter Thirty-two

When we got back to my apartment, they were waiting for us.

Thankfully, Martin had fallen asleep in my backseat on the short drive over, and didn't wake up when I parked the car.

They came at us as soon as we got out, so I left Martin inside, hoping they wouldn't see him.

We had parked beside each other, across the lot from the apartments near the basketball court. They had appeared out of the darkness, one on each end of the cars, trapping us between them.

I recognized Vincent Storr so assumed the guy he was with was Raymond Pelton.

"This him?" Ray asked.

In contrast to Vince, Ray was round and short with big, muscular arms, thick, stubby-fingered hands, no neck, and not much hair.

Vince nodded. "Motherfucker came to my job site."

The night was dark, the complex quiet, everyone behind their locked doors doing what they did when they went inside.

"Who's this pretty little piece of pussy you got here?" Ray said, eyeing Jordan lasciviously, his thick tongue molesting his lower lip as he did.

"She's got nothin' to do with this," I said. "Let her go on inside."

"I don't even like girls and I'm gonna fuck this one. Show her how good it can be up the ass."

"She's got a small one on her," Vince said. "Won't be hard to pretend she's a little boy."

How stupid could I be? Not only was this my fault, but I had put Jordan right in the middle of it.

I had no weapon of any kind, no way of defending myself, let alone her. I couldn't keep screwing up like this. I had to get better at what I was doing and fast. Of course, because of this screwup, I may not get the chance to get better.

Think. Come up with something. Fast.

"I wouldn't talk that way about a cop's wife," I said. "Only thing worse than killin' a cop is doin' anything at all to one of their wives."

"You ain't no cop," Ray said.

"No, but her husband is. Like I was saying. Messin' with her is misery like you don't need."

"You're fuckin' a cop's wife but you're tellin' us not to?" Vince said.

"I haven't touched her," I said. "I know better. Like I said, she has nothin' to do with this."

Ray seemed to consider what I had said.

"All this 'cause I'm interested in information about a kid who was killed six years ago?" I said.

"Why the interest?" Ray asked.

"We're the same age. Or would be. Could've been me."

"Still could be."

"This just doesn't make sense," I said. "Why the over-response? If you didn't kill LaMarcus, I wouldn't think you'd want to draw so much attention to yourselves. And if you did, I'd think you'd want to attract even less."

"Don't try to play me, boy," Ray said.

"I'm not. I'm serious."

"I want to be left the fuck alone," Ray said. "So I wanted

to know what little punk was comin' to Vince's job site asking after me and why."

I nodded.

"Vince, blade," Ray said.

So fast I wasn't even sure it had happened at first, Vince had an arm around Jordan's throat and the point of a knife at her neck.

I took a step toward her.

"Don't do it," Ray said. "If you do, she'll be dead before you get there."

I stopped.

"Here's what's going to happen," Ray said. "I'm gonna ask you a couple of questions. If you lie or I even think you are, she's gonna get her throat slit. Understand?"

I nodded.

"Show him we ain't fuckin' around, Vince."

Vince cut into the side of Jordan's neck a little and she screamed.

"That's nothin'," Ray said. "A little scratch. Imagine if he really went to work on her, slicing through her skin like thin sheetrock paper."

Beside the beat of my heart in my head, all I could hear were the not dissimilar sounds of the wind, the *whoosh* of traffic on I-20, and Jordan's panicked breaths.

Jordan's breathing was loud and labored. Blood was on her neck, the blade, and Vince's fingers.

"Satisfy my curiosity and you'll walk," Ray said. "Lie to me and I'll leave you both bleeding out on this asphalt."

I nodded. "Okay," I said, "but I was serious about her being a cop's wife."

He looked at Jordan. "What's your husband's name? Where's he work? What's his badge number?"

She told him in a trembly voice. She sounded scared but as if she was telling the truth.

As she spoke, I stole a glance at Martin. He was beginning to stir. It wouldn't be long before he was awake and climbing out of the car right into this.

Ray nodded and looked back at me. "Why are you looking into what happened to that kid?"

"It started when I was a lot younger," I said. "I met Wayne Williams, became obsessed with the case. Well, I already was, but that really sealed it for me. I've studied the Atlanta Child Murders my whole life—or what seems like it. I came to LaMarcus through them, to see if he was one of the killer's victims—*that* killer's. When I met the family and saw all they had been through . . . I just wanted . . . to help. To try to find out who killed LaMarcus and why. That's it."

He nodded.

"What's her connection?" he asked, jerking his head toward Jordan.

"She's his sister. His stepsister."

"She really married to a cop?"

I nodded.

"You really not bangin' her?"

"I'm really not."

"But you want to be?"

"I do."

"Whatta you think, Vince? He tellin' the truth?"

"Can never go wrong by cuttin', Ray," Vince said.

Ray shook his head. "I'm sorry about your brother," he said to Jordan, "but I didn't kill him—or any other kids. I swear it. And I want to be left out of it. For all sorts of reasons. Not least of which is other things I got goin' right now. Look for whoever snuffed your brother, just leave me out of it. And make sure your husband and your boyfriend here do too. If y'all do, you'll never see me again. If you don't, I swear to Christ Vince will cut your tits off and mail one to your husband and one to this boy who wants to be bangin' you. And that'll just be for starters. Nod if you understand."

She did.

"Both of you."

I nodded too.

"Nod if you're going to leave me the fuck out of all this."

We both nodded.

"Only get one chance. No bullshit. No warnings. No mercy. And we won't just kill you. We'll do things to you first, things that'll make you wish we had just killed you. Cop's wife or not. Won't matter."

Without another word or gesture, Ray turned and walked away.

Vince shoved Jordan into me, licked her blood off his blade, and followed.

Chapter Thirty-three

"Are you okay?" I asked.

She nodded.

She was shaking and seemed in shock.

I was holding her, trying to hug her fear and trauma away, but needed to look at her neck.

"How's your neck?" I asked. "Let me . . ."

I pulled back a little to examine her neck but it was too dark and she didn't want to let go.

"Come on," I said. "Let's go inside and get you taken care of.

Without letting go of her, I eased over and awkwardly opened the door, woke Martin up, and helped him out of the car.

"Sorry, buddy, but you're gonna have to walk. Can't carry you tonight."

He looked up at me sleepily, nodded, then stumbled out of the car, across the lot, and up the steps with us.

It took a little doing—we moved like the infirmed and inebriated attempting a three-legged race—but eventually we were in my room, Martin on a pallet on the floor, Jordan in my bed.

She was still trembling and her small hand was pressed against her neck.

"I need to look at it," I said.

I grabbed her wrist to ease her hand back. There was something erotic about the gesture, electric, and I wondered if she felt it too, or would have had she been able to.

She seemed to come out of her shock a bit and smiled up at me. "I like that."

"Me too."

"Sorry I'm being such a wimp."

"You're not. Not at all."

Pulling her hand back, I checked her wound. It was nearly two inches but didn't seem very deep and had pretty much stopped bleeding.

"Need to clean it," I said.

I tried to think of who might have peroxide, antibiotic ointment, and a Band-Aid, and felt like an inadequate adult for not having anything but soap, shampoo, toothpaste, deodorant, and fish sticks in the apartment.

"It's fine," she said. "Really."

Martin made a noise and shifted in his sleep and we both looked over at him.

"I'm so glad he slept through it," she said.

I nodded.

"Still can't believe it happened," she said. "Just . . . right out there . . . just . . ."

"I'm sorry," I said. "I should've never gone to see Vincent, should've never put you and Martin in a situation like that. Still can't believe I screwed up so bad. It was stupid and amateurish and I'm so sorry."

She shook her head. "You saved us," she said. "You stayed calm and you talked them out of . . . what they were going to do. They came with different intentions but you convinced Ray to alter his actions. You were . . . just to be able to stay calm and deal with the situation . . . It was impressive."

"Should've never been in that situation. Think about

what could've happened. I've got to get better at this. And quick."

"What're you gonna do?" she asked. "Did you believe him? About not havin' anything to do with what happened to LaMarcus and what he'd do to me if you . . ."

I shrugged. "Not sure how much I believe," I said. "Don't want to put you in danger like that again . . . but . . ."

"They're such . . . They seem really evil."

I nodded. "Not a lot of humanity there."

"Listen," she said. "I don't want you to worry about me. I don't want you stopping for me. I'll be fine. I'll be more careful. But I don't want you gettin' hurt . . . or . . . worse. I mean it. It won't bring LaMarcus back. It's not worth gettin' killed over."

I thought about it. Was she right? If I was going to do this, do work like this in any way, I would have to figure out what was worth dying for and what wasn't. I'd have to make peace with the possibility of an early death and then live and investigate with abandon and conviction and without fear.

"I've . . . lost so . . . much," she said. "It's really all I know."

I nodded, but didn't say anything.

"I'd like to know something else," she said. "I really would."

"I'd like that for you too."

"I . . ." she began, but trailed off and didn't return to it.

"What?" I said. "You what?"

"I . . . I feel like . . . I could know something different with you. With you and Martin. Feel like I already do."

I reached down and removed a strand of hair from her face.

She looked up at me with big green eyes that were beautiful and brilliant, shy and searching. Her beauty, which was breathtaking, snuck up on you. She looked as sweet and innocent and simple and sexy as a schoolgirl who'd yet to start fixing up for boys.

"Will you hold me?" she said.

"I will," I said, "but before I do . . . I . . . You probably don't even need me to say this . . . so I'm sayin' it for me . . . because I need to say it and I need to hear myself say it. I'm not sayin' you want to or would . . . but . . . there are certain lines I won't cross."

"Okay . . ."

"Marriage is one of them," I said.

"I had no idea you were so opposed to marriage," she said.

"No, I meant I can't sleep with—"

"I knew what you meant," she said. "You're so sweet, John. Just precious. And I already knew . . . I could tell . . . a woman can tell things about a man."

"I just . . ."

"Two things," she said. "One, I think it's time to . . . I hope not to be married much longer . . . and two," —she smiled a sweet, playful, seductive smile— "just knowin', in the poetic words of Raymond Pelton, you want to *bang me*, is enough for now."

Chapter Thirty-four

This was not going to be pleasant.

I was meeting Bobby Battle and Frank Morgan at the Waffle House on Evans Mill Road to discuss the case and all my mistakes.

We were in a booth in the back corner of the crowded restaurant, the two of them on one side of the table, me on the other.

"I don't have long," Battle said. "So . . ."

"Bobby, this young man's gonna close your case for you and you can't spare a few minutes."

"I'm here, aren't I? I'm just sayin' we need to get on with it."

I nodded.

"And," Battle added, "if this case could be closed it would be."

Frank smiled and winked at me.

"I need to start with my fuckup," I said.

"*Another one*?" Battle said.

"More of a continuation."

Battle blew out a frustrated sigh and shook his head.

"Relax, Bobby," Frank said, "you're gonna give yourself a heart attack. And then what would happen? Criminals would take over the entire town."

Battle took a sip of his coffee and seemed to settle down a bit.

The restaurant was loud, the clanking of plates, the clinking of cups, the constant hum and occasional outburst of conversation making it difficult to concentrate.

"Raymond Pelton and Vincent Storr paid me a little visit last night," I said.

I then went on to tell them most of the rest.

"Told you, didn't I?" Battle said. "Goddamn it. Frank, I told him to stay away from them. And this is why. Now you got them coming where you live to threaten you."

"Means he hit a nerve," Frank said.

"Nobody ever questioned guys like them being stirred up in all kind of bad shit. Of course they're gonna come out swingin'. Doesn't mean either of them had anything to do with what happened to LaMarcus."

"There's more," I said.

"The fuck?" Battle said. "What *more* could there be?"

"They threatened the sister."

Both men looked confused.

"LaMarcus's sister?" Battle said. "Jordan Moore? A cop's wife? Why? How would she even— Was she there? She was there with you? Are you fuckin' kiddin' me? What the *fuck* is the wife of a cop doing at your apartment, John?"

"She . . . we had just come from talking to Carlton Fields. Actually, she talked to him. I just listened."

"You've got the wife of a cop mixed up in this cluster fuck."

"Long before she married an abusive asshole cop, she was LaMarcus's stepsister. She wants to find out who killed him more than anybody."

He shook his head. I had him on that.

"Doesn't explain why she was at your apartment," he said. "Does her abusive, asshole of a husband know?"

"We were goin' to talk about what Carlton said. Which you two need to hear, by the way."

"What happened?" Bobby said. "Tell me exactly what happened—what was said, what was done, all of it, every detail."

I did.

The midday sun shone brightly through the plate glass windows that served as walls, shafts of light streaking the tile floor, emphasizing random objects indiscriminately—jukebox, bubblegum ball machine, an empty chair, a napkin holder, part of a tabletop.

"Now I'm gonna have to come down hard on Pelton and Storr," Battle was saying. "Have to find something on them to send them away for a long, long time."

"That won't be hard, Bobby," Frank said. "And you know it."

"Can't have them runnin' around threatenin' to cut the tits off a cop's wife. *Fuck*. I don't have time for this shit right now."

"I'll help you," Frank said.

"I do it and you're goin' to do two things for me," Battle said to me. "Stay out of my case and away from Larry Moore's wife."

I shook my head. "I can't," I said. "I won't."

"Are you fuckin' her?"

I shook my head again. "I'm not. And I won't."

"Come on, Bobby," Frank said. "Stop all this and let's hear what he has for us on the case. He's doin' great work, helpin' us a lot. And you know it. Nothin' was happenin' on this case and nothin' was goin' to. Show him the appreciation he deserves."

Battle shook his head. "Unbelievable. Appreciation, huh?"

"What did Carlton say?" Frank asked.

I told them.

"Said it was a secret," Frank said, "that his dad was going to come get him and take him away?"

I nodded. "And that lines up with what Anthony told me, that he'd do anything he had to to make a man out of his son."

They both seemed to think about it.

"That's good," Frank said. "Isn't it, Bobby? It's real good."

"I looked long and hard at Anthony Alex Williams, Jr. back when it happened," Battle said. "You know what really broke in his favor—I mean, apart from there being no evidence against him at all? The rape. Couldn't see him doin' all this, includin' bringin' a condom, to rape his own son. Be one thing if he lived with him or if he had any history of pedophilia, but he didn't and I just couldn't see him stagin' this whole elaborate thing to kill then rape his own son."

I nodded. "What if he didn't?"

He looked at me like I was in need of electroshock therapy. "Yeah, that's what I just said."

"What if he committed the first but not the second crime? What if he killed him—by accident—and someone else moved him and raped him? Anthony plans to come and take his son, just like he told me and LaMarcus told Carlton, but he gives him too much of the sleep aid, accidentally overdoses him. He panics. Leaves LaMarcus in the bushes. Flees. Then someone else comes along and moves the body to the drainage culvert and rapes him. That would allow for the time LaMarcus spent lying in the one position on the ground before being moved, and would mean his dad didn't rape him."

"That's good," Frank said. "Really good. That could really be it. Think about it, Bobby. That makes a lot of sense."

Battle nodded absently, his unfocussed eyes staring at nothing in the distance as his cop mind worked the theory around.

"You got anybody in mind?" Frank asked me. "For the

doer. The rapist."

I nodded. "Pelton. Storr. Carlton. Ralph Alderman."

"Alderman?" Bobby said.

I told them about Carlton's reaction to Ralph.

"Could mean nothin'," Battle said.

"But it could mean somethin'," Frank said. "It really could."

"Yeah, and it could be nothin'."

"Why did Ralph really leave the force?" I asked.

"GBI did the investigation," Battle said. "Ask him."

I looked at Frank.

"I'll find out," he said.

"And while he's doin' that, I'll try to make the world a safer place for people like you and a fellow cop's wife by cleaning the streets of Pelton and Storr. And while we do that, how about *you* don't do anything? Nothin' else to get somebody killed or fuck up my case. Okay? Except . . . get a pager so I can keep tabs on you. I'm serious. Get one today."

Chapter Thirty-five

"What the hell is wrong with you?" the small woman yelled.

She was standing at the fence in front of Safe Haven, having just screeched up in her car and stormed up to the chain-link barrier, and was yelling over it at Jordan.

Jordan and I were sitting on the center bench on the breezeway. Besides Ralph we were the only two outside. It would be another twenty minutes or so until the kids crashed the playground.

"Oh no," Jordan said.

"Who is it?"

"Carlton's mom," she said. "Vanessa."

So short she could barely see over the fence, the tiny woman had straight black hair and a darkish complexion that made her look part Native-American.

"How could you . . ." Vanessa was saying.

Ralph was moving in her direction but from inside the fence.

"You stay the hell away from me you evil son of a—"

"Vanessa," Jordan said as we reached her. "What's going on? What is it? Why're you doing this?"

"How could you, Jordan?" she said.

"How could I what?"

"You're supposed to protect children, especially the ones like Carlton."

"Ma'am, I'm gonna have to ask you to leave," Ralph was saying.

His shaky voice betrayed his nervousness, and though it was a cool morning, his shirt was now soaked through with sweat.

"Get this fat piece of shit away from me right now," Vanessa said, "or I swear to God I'll have this place shut down by nightfall."

"Give us a minute, Ralph," Jordan said.

"But—"

"Now."

"Yes, ma'am," he said, backing away. "I'll be right over here if you—"

"Ralph," she said, "stop talking and go. Now."

He did, backing away awkwardly over to his sentry post position near the main gate.

"I can't believe you let that fat creepy bastard around my son."

"I didn't. I mean . . . not on purpose. And all he did was see him for a second from about twenty-five feet away."

"Well that was enough to upset him as bad as I've ever seen him . . . except when . . . your . . . brother died."

"My brother didn't just die. He was the victim of a violent murder."

"And you've got the man who most likely did it working for you, supposedly protecting other children. You bring him around my son. What the fuck is wrong with you?"

The conversation wasn't pleasant, but the day was. Cool, crisp air, no humidity, orange and brown burnished leaves emblazoned on the trees, and the overall good feeling of fall.

"Why is Carlton so afraid of Ralph?" I asked.

"Fat bastard terrorized the hell out of them when they were little."

I couldn't imagine Carlton ever being little, which was somewhat odd to think because his mom was an extremely petite woman, smaller even than Jordan.

"How?"

"In a thousand different ways. He bullied the bejesus out of them. Made them do things. He's creepy as hell. Never have been able to get the full story out of Carlton, but it was bad."

"I had no idea," Jordan said.

"Are you serious? How could you not know something like that? How could you have him working here? What the hell kind of haven you running here? Sure as shit ain't safe."

"Did you bully my brother?" Jordan asked Ralph.

The moment Vanessa had turned to leave, we had walked directly over to where he stood.

"What? No. Is that what that crazy bitch said?"

"Whoa," I said.

"Watch it with that, Ralph," Jordan said.

"Sorry, but . . . it's insane."

"It's not insane," I said. "You're a bully."

"I'm not. I've never . . . All I did was teach them some discipline. That's it. Neither of them had a dad around. I was the only man in their lives, the only adult to take an interest in them, in how they turned out, in what kind of men they would become."

"You never touched them?" I said.

"*What? No.* Oh God, no. See? I told you. If she said that then she's insane. I swear to God. I never. That's so sick. I would never. Not ever. Not anybody."

He was in full panic mode—red faced, raised, tight, shrill voice, wide, wild eyes.

"Did you kill LaMarcus?" Jordan asked.

"*Jordan*," he said, his wounded voice as saddened as

shocked. "Of course not. How could you even ask. I never laid a finger on him. Never. I didn't bully him or hurt him or Carlton in any way. Not ever. I swear to God. Strap me up to a polygraph right now. I'm tellin' the truth. I swear it."

Ida sat quietly thinking for a long moment, chewing her lip as she did, her brow furrowed, her eyes narrowed in concentration.

Jordan had just finished telling her what Vanessa had accused Ralph of and Ralph's response.

Kids and staff out on the playground under the watchful gaze of Ralph Alderman, the three of us were alone inside the large, empty main room of the daycare center.

The room smelled of sleep and sweat, of glue and paint, of cleaning chemicals and air freshener, every surface moist and sticky.

"Whatta you think I should do, John?" she asked. "Let him go right now? Give him a chance to respond? Try to line up a polygraph?"

I shrugged.

Before I could answer, she added, "I'd find it very hard to fire a man over an accusation. I mean, that's all we have, right? He's never given me one minute of trouble. He's overzealous sometimes, but that's it."

"It'd be nice to be able to have him here so we could watch him," I said. "Dig a little deeper into his life while keeping an eye on him, but . . . the stakes are just too high."

"You think it's possible he killed my boy?"

I nodded. "It's possible he had something to do with what happened to LaMarcus—even if someone else was involved too."

"Someone else?"

"We think it's at least possible that two people were involved."

"Well find out fast," she said. "'Cause I can't fire a good employee and family friend because of an accusation."

"I will," I said, thinking that if I didn't and something happened to one of the kids in their care . . .

Chapter Thirty-six

"You okay?" Frank Morgan asked.

I was walking to my car when he pulled into the Safe Haven parking lot and rolled down his passenger side window.

I shrugged.

"Get in," he said.

I did.

"When's the last time you've eaten?"

"Not sure. Last night I guess. But I'm okay."

"Let's grab a burger. We'll just run through a drive-thru. Eat in the car. I'll bring you right back here in a few minutes."

"I'm not hungry," I said. "But you eat. I'll go along for the ride."

"How much money you got?" he asked.

"On me? None. But . . ."

"But," he said, "somewhere else you have plenty?"

"Well, not plenty, but . . ."

"Any?"

I nodded.

"How much? And don't lie to me."

"Gas money for the rest of the week."

"That much, huh? So you can get where you need to go—including work and working this case and Grady to help someone else, but you can't eat if you do."

"I can eat. I'm eating."

"Here's what's gonna happen," he said. "I'm gonna buy you one of these awful Cindy's burgers up here and you're gonna eat it just like it's decent. Then I'm gonna give you this crisp fifty dollar bill in my wallet and you're gonna eat the rest of this week—every day, hell, twice a day—and the only thing you're going to say is what you like on your burger. Understand?"

I had to swallow hard against the lump in my throat and blink back the tears stinging my eyes.

The relief I felt was indescribable.

"Thank you, Frank."

"Thank you Frank is not a condiment. Tell me what you want on your knockoff burger."

"It means more than you'll ever know."

"It's just food. It's not love."

"The hell it's not," I said. "The hell it's not."

He pulled up and we ordered. While we waited, advancing around the building one car length at a time every few minutes, he handed me the fifty out of his wallet and said, "So now that your money troubles are temporarily over, tell me what's bothering you."

"This case. When I'm not making rookie mistakes, I'm not gettin' anywhere. I suck at this. And that's not just a shame because this is what I want to do with my life, but because somebody really needs to find out who killed LaMarcus and do something about it."

He nodded. We finally got our food and we pulled back out onto the road.

"Thing is," I said, "I have too *many* not too few suspects. I can't exclude anyone."

"Often the case," he said. "Tell you what . . . between bites of that burger, why don't you walk me through it."

I did.

"I can see it being one perp or two," I said. "I can see it

being the biological father or Pelton or Storr or Alderman or Carlton or some combination of them—one to do the killing, another the rape, but . . . I can't exclude any of them. Hell, I can't even completely rule out Wayne Williams. It's driving me crazy."

He nodded, his expression telling me he knew exactly what I meant.

"It's that way far more often than you'd think," he said. "Sometimes there's several people who could've done it and you can't pinpoint which one. Others you know exactly who did it and just can't prove it. And far too often you can never be certain about exactly what happened or who did what. Think about Wayne Williams. I'm pretty sure he's the Atlanta Child Murderer, but I'm not certain. You've looked at most of the evidence and you're not certain one way or the other. It's the job. Can you reconcile ambiguity? Can you live with not knowing? Move on."

"I don't know that I can."

"You can live with far more than you think you can," he said. "You'll learn that soon enough."

It was maybe the first time he'd treated me like anything other than a peer. I didn't like it. He was probably right. I was pretty sure he was. But that didn't mean I had to like it.

We ate in silence a few moments as he drove back down Flat Shoals toward Safe Haven.

"You know," he said, "it's at least possible that the doer is someone else entirely."

"Why I'm not gonna stop looking," I said.

"Never doubted that," he said. "Not for a minute."

Chapter Thirty-seven

"I would've committed suicide if it weren't for this group," a nervous, emaciated, sunbaked young woman said. "I'm not just being melodramatic. I mean it. If I didn't have you guys . . . if I didn't have this work to do . . ."

"It works if you work it," an older man with a wet, gurgley smoker's voice said. "You did the work. We just supported you."

I had come with Jordan and Ida to the support group for grieving parents held in a meeting room of the K Center at Chapel Hill.

It was facilitated by George Clarke, a tall, thin, soft-spoken African-American pastor in a navy-blue suit and burgundy clerical collar.

"Grief is a natural response to loss," Pastor George had said. "It's the emotional suffering you feel when something or someone you love is taken away. The more significant the loss, the more intense the grief will be. And there's no loss like the loss of a child. No pain like it. Nothin' compares. There's nothin' more personal or individual than the process of grieving. There's no one single way to do it. There are no steps. No rules. No particular timeframe. But there are common stages and ways of coping and dealing and healing that work far better than others. And most important . . . is having a support system.

That's why we're here."

After those introductory remarks and a reminder of the group's ground rules, each member took a turn sharing.

"You get to a point where loss and pain and grief are all you know," Jordan said.

It was Jordan's turn.

She looked at me. "Someone decent and good and kind comes along, something good happens in your life, and you don't even know how to process it, but you realize if you don't, if you don't recognize the good when it comes along, if you don't receive it, then you've lost, trauma and tragedy have won, have gotten the last word. You realize that you might as well have died when your child did, because what you're doing is not living, is not life."

Several people nodded, but a few others, others probably more recently entering the grief process, still raw, weren't as sure.

"We don't want to live," she said. "We feel not just sad, not just broken from the unimaginable loss, unthinkable undoing of our very existences, we feel guilty. Guilty for being here, for being alive, guilt that is compounded and multiplied by anything with even the possibility of leading to something like joy or pleasure or even the slight lightening of the load of pain we bear."

Jordan was in her element here. She knew loss. She knew pain. She knew grief. And she spoke more eloquently about it, and with more wisdom and profundity, than in any other situation I had seen her in or on any other topic I had witnessed her address.

Next up was a youngish, buttoned-up black man with glasses and an honest to God pocket protector. "I was reading *Crime and Punishment* this week and came across this— 'The darker the night, the brighter the stars, the deeper the grief, the closer is God.' When I first read it I really liked it. Even highlighted it and wrote it down. But the more I read it, the more I just wasn't sure. I mean . . . is it true? Doesn't really seem true except maybe for some of the time."

"God is close to a broken heart," an elderly black lady said, "an ever present help in our time of need."

"Those are just platitudes," the professorial-looking man said. "Just 'cause someone said it doesn't make it true."

"It's in the Bible," she said. "That's what makes it true."

"I'll tell you what's true," a middle-aged white man said. "Pain. Pain is truth. It's so true sometimes there seems like there's nothin' else. I just . . . I'm not sure I can keep going like this, feeling like this. I'm not sure I even want to."

"I didn't just lose a child," Ida said when it was her turn. "I lost a grandchild too. My son was the victim of violence and I still don't know who did it. There's no . . . Talk about pain. Talk about darkness and a demon that won't leave you alone. Then to see your grandchild suffer for all of her short life and then die . . . It's too much. It doesn't ever go away. Not ever. But it does become just barely bearable. Just barely. It does. Trust me. Hang on. Don't give up."

"Why?" the middle-aged white man asked. "So I can get to barely bearable? That's what I have to look forward to? That's not enough."

Sitting among the ruins, listening to the raw bone pain pour out, feeling the overwhelming oppression of loss and grief, despair and hopelessness, I realized just how little loss I had undergone, just how pain free my relatively easy existence had been thus far, and on top of every other difficult emotion I was experiencing, I also felt guilt.

"I don't see how y'all do it," I said to Ida and Jordan after the group had concluded, its members dispersed back to the despair that was the norm of their lives.

We were walking down the long, light blue-carpeted hallway of the K Center toward the door.

"To live with the . . . with what you do . . . then to . . .

take in all the pain and grief of the group. It just seems . . . too much."

"Sometimes it is," Ida said.

"It really does help to share it," Jordan said. "To feel heard and understood, to get to give that back to others in a similar situation."

I wondered which I could do to help more people—ministry or investigation. How could I combine my interests, talents, and opportunities to make some small difference in the time and place and circumstance I was born into.

"Thank you again for all you're doin' for us," Ida said. "You can't know what it means, how it helps, but . . ."

I waited, unable to imagine what was coming next.

"We lived this way a long time. We gonna get by. Don't you be puttin' too much undo pressure on yourself."

I must have inadvertently expressed I wasn't following.

"We don't have any expectations," Jordan said. "We've resigned ourselves to not knowing what happened to LaMarcus and why."

"Well, I haven't," I said. "I can't. I won't."

"'For now we see through a glass, darkly,'" Ida said, quoting Saint Paul, "'but then face to face: now I know in part; but then shall I know even as also I am known.' Sometimes we just don't get to know."

"I can't accept that," I said.

She shook her head and frowned.

"You live long enough, you'll learn to."

Chapter Thirty-eight

Later that afternoon, Bishop Paulk's secretary, Dottie Bridges, had called the college and asked me to come to the bishop's office as soon as I had finished cleaning the classrooms.

I arrived in the dimming, dusky early evening to find Bishop Paulk and Pastor Don waiting for me.

The entire K Center was quiet, the other offices empty, the rest of the staff having gone home for the day.

As usual, both men were in suits and full clerical collars.

Having just come from work, I was in faded jeans, a gray Magic Johnson sweatshirt, and a pair of New Balance Worthy 790s with purple and yellow Laker color highlights, and I felt underdressed and out of place.

They were friendly and welcoming and asked about my classes and work at EPI and my life in general, Bishop Paulk behind his enormous desk, Pastor Don and I in the two chairs across the desk from him.

"How's your investigation going?" Don asked.

I told them.

"You must really be getting somewhere with it," he said. "Getting close to the killer."

"What makes you say that?"

"We received another call from someone claiming to be the killer," Earl Paulk said.

"Really?" I asked, my mind racing. "Wow. That's . . . Was it the same guy?"

"I can't be sure," he said. "It's been a long time. But . . . I just don't know. It could be, but he sounded different somehow."

I nodded and thought about it. "Of course it could be unrelated to anything I've done."

"Actually, he mentioned you by name," he said.

"Really?"

I just thought my mind was racing before.

Who could it be? I had talked to so many possible suspects. Was it one of them or someone I wasn't even aware of?

"What did he say?"

"That he had called me before, that he needed help, that he wanted to stop, that you were stirring it all up for him and the memories were haunting him and he couldn't take it."

I thought about who I had spoken with that would know of my connection to Chapel Hill and Bishop Paulk.

"You have any idea who it could be?" Don asked. "Got a leading suspect?"

"Not really, no."

"What would you do if you were given the chance to talk to him?" Earl asked.

I noticed he asked what would I do not what would I say, and I wondered if that was intentional.

"What would I do?"

"How would you handle it?"

I really didn't know. I had imagined various scenarios, of course, but not very seriously, not in any but the most fantastical ways.

"I'm not sure exactly."

"Would you talk to him as an investigator or as a minister?"

"I don't know. I . . . Honestly, I often find myself torn between the two, but . . ."

"Are you more interested in temporary justice or his eternal soul?"

I knew the answer immediately, but took a beat to give it because I didn't want to sound flippant. "Both," I said.

"There's got to be a place for both," Don said.

"I hope so."

"But when they're at odds," Earl said, "which will you choose?"

I didn't respond, just thought about it.

"I'm a minister," he said. "First. Last. Always. I want to help him if I can."

I nodded.

"He says he's gonna kill again if he doesn't get help."

My heart started pounding even harder.

"You interested in helping me help him?"

I said I was, but thought we might have differing ideas of what that meant exactly.

"He said he'd come see us—you, me, and Pastor Don—if and only if all three of us were here. And no one else was. No cops. No staff. No one. Only us. He said for us to be here at the church every night this week and when he was ready and convinced there were no cops, he'd come by and talk to us."

The excitement shooting through me was like a drug. I couldn't believe this was happening. This was why I was here—the earlier phone calls to Bishop Paulk the reason I was standing in his office at this moment.

"You willing to stay with us here tonight and every night this week until he shows?" Don asked.

I was nodding before he was even close to finishing the question.

I'd have to figure out a way of getting Martin fed, and I'd miss my time with Jordan, but this was something I had to do.

"And to be here as a churchman and not a lawman," Earl said.

I wasn't either. Not really. But I knew what he meant,

and I nodded, though it was somewhat disingenuous. Whatever I was, whatever words fit better than churchman and lawman, I could never be either or, never be only one or the other, and I suspected he knew it.

"We're not saying you can't be who you are," Don said. "Just that you understand and respect what we're about. We're going to do our best to get him to turn himself in—"

"But we're not setting a trap for him," Earl said. "Not going to try to make an arrest ourselves and we don't want you to."

"I understand."

Sitting quietly in the enormous empty building waiting for a killer to call was creepy and unnerving.

Earlier in the evening, Norma Paulk, the bishop's wife, had brought us dinner. After eating, we had settled in to wait—sitting, standing, walking around the office.

Waiting.

For the first few hours, we had talked about the case and Kingdom Theology and the challenges I would face attempting to do both ministry and law enforcement. Later, we had each pulled a book from the shelf and read in silence. Now we just sat and waited.

I had been unable to communicate with Martin or Jordan and I wondered if they were worried.

No call came that first night.

At a little after two in the morning on the second night, the killer called back and said he wasn't coming that night either, but that he had been watching and was encouraged to see that we had not involved the cops. If that continued he'd come see us soon.

Weary and welcoming the release, we rushed out quickly toward the opportunity to get some actual sleep in our beds, and it wasn't until after the Paulks had left together that I remembered I had parked on the side of the building—something I had done for a few minutes privacy with Jordan before going in.

The night was dark and quiet, very little visible back here, no sound but that of the wind.

Beneath thick clouds that covered the moon and the stars nothing stirred, nothing contradicted my sense of utter isolation.

As I walked around the back of the enormous K Center in the blackness of the night, I kept imagining the killer jumping out of the darkness to strangle or stab or rape or brain me, and I could feel the fear starting to seize me up, mind and body.

The grass of the hilly ground was damp with dew, the soft sounds of my footfalls barely perceptible, but I thought for sure I heard others in the short distance over my right shoulder.

There's no one there. It's just your imagination, your fear. Don't look. Just keep walking.

Unable to help myself, I spun around and scanned the area as best I could.

No one was there that I could make out, but I could only see a short distance into the dark.

Turning back around, I picked up my pace, walking so fast it was nearly a run.

My footfalls were louder now.

And so were the others. Or the others I thought I heard.

I wanted to run but was unable to do anything other than was I was doing.

When I reached the edge of the building, the vast parking lot was visible—hundreds and hundreds of empty spots and there in the not too far distance a lone automobile, appearing eerie and abandoned.

As frightened as I had been back behind the K Center in the dark, I realized that I was far more vulnerable in the long lighted walk across the lot.

I pictured predator and prey on a shimmering African plain—a small gazelle separated from the herd, a sleek cheetah, the fastest land animal on the planet, designed for this, for the chase, for the kill.

Feeling far more exposed than at any other time in my entire life, I stumbled down the hill and began my trek toward my vehicle.

Not far into it, I began to jog. Not long after that, I began to run.

Glancing over my shoulder often, scanning the area all around me as best I could, I ran awkwardly, unsteadily, disjointedly, my body stiff with fear, my blood thick with adrenaline.

It wasn't until I was well into my run that I noticed the other car in the lot.

About a hundred feet away in the far rear corner, a black Oldsmobile Cutlass with darkly tinted windows had been backed into the parking spot, its nose pointing toward my car, a tiny trail of exhaust rising up and vanishing into the night air behind it.

I was too close to the car to turn around, but even if I hadn't been, the church building behind me was locked, unable to provide any sanctuary.

I ran even faster.

I could feel myself losing my balance, about to trip, to fall face first into the ungiving asphalt.

But somehow I managed to stay on my faltering feet.

As I ran, I continued to scan the entire area, but most of my focus and mental energy was trained on the Cutlass, which had yet to move.

When I finally made it to my car and was safely inside, I felt foolish, but not foolish enough not to check my backseat and speed away, my eyes darting to my rearview mirror often as

I did—particularly toward the parking spot in the back of the lot where the dark car still mercifully remained.

The call came at midnight on the third night.

The loud, abrupt ring piercing the silence, startling.

Bishop Paulk's voice was dry and quiet and sounded sleepy.

My pulse kicked into overdrive, adrenaline spiking into the red, my mind reeling.

Am I really this close to the killer?

"There's no one here but us," Earl was saying into the phone. "You have my word. I even sent our security guard home for the evening . . . It's not a trap . . . I want to help you. That's all I'm interested in. I want you to know God loves you no matter what you've done . . . No, I . . . I do. I truly believe that."

I stood and began moving around a bit.

"Yes, he's here. Don too."

Bishop grew quiet, listening to what I assumed were our instructions.

"We'll do that. Just like you said, but I don't want anyone getting hurt. We're operating in good faith. Are you doing the same?"

He waited.

"Why not meet with all three of us? Or let John and Pastor Don go home and just meet with me . . . Okay. Just don't hurt those who're trying to help you."

When the bishop hung up, he kept his hand on the receiver for a long moment, seemingly contemplating the conversation.

"Well?" Don said.

"He wants us to split up. One at each door. Wants to make sure we don't gang up on him. He'll approach one of us and if he's comfortable, whoever he chooses can lead him to the other two."

"He's just separating us so he can pick us off one at a time."

"Why? Why would he do that? He says we're to stand at three different doors but that we can keep the doors locked so we can see him approaching and know it's not an ambush."

"Something's just not right about it," Don said.

"He kills children," Earl said. "He's probably not a threat to us, but even if he is, we've got to try to stop him. God will be with us."

"What do you think, John?" Don asked.

"That you're both right. Something's definitely not right, but we can't let that stop us from trying to stop him."

"Why is he really separating us?" Don said.

"It could be what he said, but . . . I think it's far more likely that he has another motive. What if he's not really wanting help at all? What if he thinks I'm getting too close, thinks I know more than I do, and he's really just trying to get me alone."

"That makes far more sense," Don said. "Would explain why he wanted you here."

"Don and I can just go down," Earl said.

I shook my head. "I think we should do it just like he said to. There's no way I can just stay up here. If there's even a chance to talk to him, to . . . I've got to try. We can be extra careful and keep the doors locked until we see him."

Bishop Paulk stood, withdrew a key from his desk, and handed it to me. "He wants you at the front door, in the vestibule near the bookstore, me in the back, and Don on the side. Don't take any chances. Be safe. Don't open the door until he shows you he's unarmed. Let's pray before we go."

The three of us joined hands and the bishop prayed for our protection and that we might help the man God was bringing to us tonight.

I slowly walked down the dark, empty hallway of the K Center toward the front door far more afraid than I could ever remember being before.

I was inspired by Earl and Don's bravery, and I was excited about the possibility of confronting one of the killers who had haunted me for so long, but more than anything I was scared. So scared I shook with it.

The only illumination came from the blood-red glow of the illuminated Exit signs and the power indicator of the emergency backup lights.

The enormous building, which held thousands for worship services and really did resemble an airplane hanger, felt vacuous, its continuous creaks echoing through the emptiness, reminding me how very alone I was.

I moved gradually, gripping the key like a weapon, edging toward the front and my fate.

Who was waiting for me? Was it LaMarcus's killer? Pelton? Storr? Anthony Alex Williams, Jr? Ralph Alderman? Maybe it really was the killer and maybe I had no idea who he was.

Up ahead, about another two hundred feet or so, I could see just a bit less dimness, as ambient lighting from outside found its way through the glass doors and into the vestibule.

As I drew closer, inch by inch, step by step, I felt more and more dread bearing down on me, heavy, oppressive, suffocating.

When I was less than a hundred feet away, I said a prayer of my own. Please protect me. Don't let me die just as my life is getting started. Please help me catch LaMarcus's killer.

Reaching the vestibule, I reminded myself—the doors are locked. Don't get too close to them. Stand sideways. Move about. Don't be an easy target. Keep your eyes wide and unfocused. Alert on movement.

Passing by the huge staircase that led up to the balcony, I moved toward the doors a little quicker now that there was a little more light.

When I reached the doors, I checked each one to ensure they were locked. Jerking hard on each one, I confirmed that I was locked inside, that at least glass doors separated me from—

And then he was on me.

Coming up from behind, snatching me back, slinging me to the ground, pulling me back into the darkness.

On top of me now. Weight pressing down. Large hunting knife with serrated blade at my throat.

"Move a muscle and I'll slit your fuckin' throat," he hissed in a low, mean whisper.

He wore a transparent plastic mask with female features and big bright makeup—round pink dots on the cheeks, pouty red pucker at the lips, thick blue swaths beneath thick black eyebrows.

The plastic facade was made all the more frightening for its lack of expression.

Behind the feminine mask, his masculine features and five o'clock shadow looked eerie and creepy and twisted.

"See how easy it is for me to get to you," he said in a hoarse whisper. "How easily I could kill you. Right now. With just the slightest flick of my wrist, twist of my blade."

I didn't respond.

"Nod if you know I could kill you quickly, quietly, and easily right now."

I nodded, careful not to move my neck too much.

"Go back to where you came from. Quit dredging up the past. Stay away from us, stay out of shit that's got nothin' to do with you. Understand? Next time . . . there won't be a next time. You'll just be dead. So will someone you care about. For her sake stop being stupid and move along."

Suddenly, and seemingly out of nowhere, Earl Paulk, shoulder lowered, plowed into the man and knocked him off me.

When the man hit the ground, he rolled, then adroitly jumped up and began running down the opposite hallway from the one I and the bishop had come down.

He hit Don, who was coming up from that direction, knocking him to the ground.

Don got up as quickly as he could and gave chase, but came back a little while later, having been unable to catch the man.

"Y'all okay?" Don asked.

We nodded.

"You?" Earl asked.

He nodded.

"Guess we both had the idea to come check on you about the same time," Earl said.

Don smiled and nodded, then turned to me. "What did he say to you?"

"Told me how easy it would be for him to kill me and said that's exactly what he would do if I didn't go back to where I came from and leave everything here alone."

"Any idea who it was?" Earl asked.

I shook my head. "Not really. If I had to guess—and that's truly all it is, a guess—I'd say a cop named Larry Moore."

Chapter Thirty-nine

A few days later, Martin and I were playing basketball when Bobby Battle sped into the apartment complex in his unmarked car, not slowing down until he reached the parking area nearest the courts.

Jordan, Martin, and I had fallen into a routine of sorts—Martin and I playing basketball in the afternoon, the three of us getting dinner of some kind, renting a movie at the video store next to the supermarket, and hanging out when Jordan was off and Larry was at work, then, after Martin fell asleep, Jordan and I alone, holding each other through the late, lonely hours of the night.

We had become something like a family. Maybe even something just like it. And Atlanta was feeling a lot like home. A lot like it.

"Keep workin' on your jump shot, buddy," I said to Martin. "I'll be back in a minute."

I walked over toward Battle, meeting him about halfway between his car and the courts.

We were well into September now and the autumnal air was cool and a bit breezy, so unlike my part of Florida this time of year.

"Thought I told you to get a pager?" Battle said.

"You did."

"Well?"

"I did."

"Where is it?" he asked.

"In my room."

"Only works if you have it on you," he said. "Keep it on you. I've been tryin' to get in touch with you for a hell of a long time."

"Okay. Sorry. I will. What's wrong?"

"Ray and Vince are in the wind."

"What?" I asked, looking around the complex before I realized what I was doing.

"We've been keepin' tabs on 'em, tryin' to catch 'em at somethin' we can come down hard on 'em for . . . and they just vanished."

I shook my head. "*Shit.*"

"I thought maybe they had you," he said. "So keep the goddamn pager on you at all times, okay?"

"Okay."

"We're lookin' for them," he said. "Hopefully we'll have 'em soon. But for now . . . lay low and keep your pager on and with you at all times."

"I will. Sorry."

"Just tryin' to look out for you. All part of the service."

"Were they under surveillance three nights ago?" I asked. "The entire night."

"Yeah. Why?"

I told him what had happened at the K Center a few nights back.

"The fuck is wrong with you, John? We had a chance to get him and you didn't even bother to tell us. Y'all could've been killed."

"I know. I just . . . I . . . Lettin' you know wasn't an option."

"You need to pick a side, John," he said. "I mean . . .

goddamn . . . You can't keep . . ."

He trailed off and we were silent a moment.

"You think it was one of them?" he asked.

"Wondered if it could've been," I said.

"Maybe it was," he said. "Maybe one slipped away while the other made it seem like they were together. I'll have to check with the surveillance team. You really think it could be one of them?"

I shrugged. "At the time I thought it was Larry Moore."

"What? Seriously? 'Cause you're fuckin' his wife? Now ain't that a whole other cluster fuck. Son, you know how to make some shit complicated, don't you?"

"I'm not sleeping with his wife," I said. "But I notice you're not sayin' he's not capable of somethin' like that."

"What? Tryin' to scare you away from his pretty little wife? 'Cause I could see his dumb ass doin' somethin' like that. It's over the top and stupid as hell, but . . . What I can't see him doin' is actually killin' you. But . . . fuck . . . let me go see what I can find out."

He turned to head back toward his car, then stopped, spun back around. "And John, look how exposed you are out here like this," he said, sweeping his arm in a broad gesture that encompassed the basketball court. "And with the kid. What're you thinkin'? You tryin' to get him killed too?"

After tucking Martin away safely, I called Jordan to warn her about Ray and Vince, but she wasn't at Safe Haven and neither was Ida, and all the woman working knew was that they had taken some time off—Jordan all day, Ida only the evening.

I called Ida's home next. There was no answer.

I wondered if I should call Jordan at home. What if Larry answered? What if all I did was make things far worse for her than they already were?

I thought about it for a long while, eventually reaching the conclusion that with Ray and Vince unaccounted for, I had to take the chance.

I let the phone ring for a very long time but no one answered.

And then I . . . I didn't know what to do.

What could I do? I was completely powerless. I had no idea where she was or if she was okay. I had no way to contact her, to check on her, to see if Ray and Vince had her at this very moment or if she was just shopping for supplies for Safe Haven with Ida.

Think, I told myself. There's got to be something. You've got to figure out something. Come on.

Two things came to mind. I could go to Safe Haven and talk to Ralph. If anyone knew where Ida and Jordan were or were supposed to be, it would be him. Or I could call Bobby Battle.

I decided to do both.

First I called Battle.

"Jordan Moore is not at work and I can't find her," I said. "Same for Ida Williams. Is Larry on duty? Can you check on her? Find out discretely if he knows where she is? Do you think Ray and Vince could have her?"

"I'm on it," he said, and hung up.

As I was about to leave for Safe Haven to see if Ralph might be willing to part with any information he might have about the whereabouts of Jordan and Ida, my phone rang.

Roger Lawson had taken a turn for the worse and was asking to see me.

Driving far faster than I should on west I-20 toward downtown and Grady, I could only worry about Jordan, only hope she was okay, only hope Bobby Battle would make sure she was.

Actually, those weren't the only things I could do.

I could also pray. I could choose to trust. I could accept

the things I couldn't change. I could change the things I could. I could find peace by acknowledging my powerlessness, serenity by letting go.

So I did—or tried to, reaching for the random blue Sparrow cassette on the backseat. As if an answer to prayer, it was Steve Camp's *One on One* and it was cued up to the beginning of "He's All You Need," which helped me find a fragile but very present peace as I sped toward downtown Atlanta.

Chapter Forty

"I'm scared," Roger Lawson said, his feeble voice no more than a hoarse, low, whistley whisper.

I nodded. "I know," I said. "And it's okay to be. It's natural. But you have nothin' to be afraid of."

I was standing beside his bed, holding his hand, leaning over, my face just inches from his.

"There's nothing but love waiting on you," I said.

"Are you sure?"

"I am. It's the only thing I'm sure of."

"I don't want to die, damn it," he said.

I nodded. "I know. I'm so, so sorry."

"Help me. Do something. I can't . . . this can't be it."

I thought back to my earlier prayer on I-20 and said, "God, grant us the serenity to accept the things we cannot change. The courage to change the things we can. And wisdom to know the difference."

He squeezed my hand.

"Say it with me," I said. "God . . . God, grant us the serenity to accept the things we cannot change. The courage to change the things we can. And wisdom to know the difference."

We said it several times together, until it became like a mantra, until peace entered the room, until he fell asleep. Peaceful sleep.

As he slept, I continued to hold his hand and say the prayer, repeating different forms, expanding, repeating.

"God, give us grace to accept with serenity the things that cannot be changed. Courage to change the things that should be changed. And the wisdom to distinguish the one from the other. Living one day at a time, enjoying one moment at a time, accepting hardship as a pathway to peace. Taking, as Jesus did, this sinful world as it is, not as we would have it be. Trusting that you will make all things right if we surrender to your will. So that we may be reasonably happy in this life and supremely happy with you forever in the next."

I continued praying for peace as Roger continued sleeping peacefully, continued until my mouth was dry and my hand ached, until he stopped breathing and the peace he was experiencing went way beyond sleep, beyond mortal, beyond the beyond and into what dreams may come.

Long after the nurses came, long after the tubes had been removed and the machines turned off, I was still praying the prayer of peace.

As I walked down the central corridor of the cold, sterile hospital, I felt sad and alone, helpless and hopeless.

And then I saw Ida and some of the pain and sadness abated.

In an instant I no longer felt alone, my spirits buoyed a bit before I realized what her presence her must mean.

"John," she said. "How'd you hear?"

"Hear what? What is it? Where's Jordan?"

"She's . . ."

"What happened? Is she—"

"She's . . . Come on. I'll take you to her."

She led me back down the corridor and along another to the emergency room and the small curtained area Jordan was waiting in.

When she saw me, she burst into tears.

"Wait here with her while I go get the car," Ida said. "Had to park in Timbuktu."

I rushed over to Jordan's bed.

"Oh, John," she said. "I'm . . . I'm so . . . so glad you're here. I'm . . . I don't know what to say."

"Start with what happened."

Her arm was in a sling, her wrist in a brace. Her face was swollen, red, and puffy around her eyes, one of which was quickly turning black.

"It's just sprained, not broken. Doesn't matter now. You're here. That's all that matters."

"Who was it?" I asked. "Who did it?"

She looked confused.

"Who?"

"Larry," she said. "Who else."

"Thought it might have been Ray and Vince."

She shook her head. "No, but . . ."

"What?"

"He knows about them," she said. "I don't know how. But he claims he's gonna kill them."

"What all'd you tell him?"

"Nothin'. John, I haven't told him anything about anything. That's what I got this for. It's got to be Battle. Brothers in blue and all that shit."

"I'm so glad you're okay," I said. "I was so worried and—"

"Me too. You're all I've been able to think about. I can't believe you're here. How are you?"

I told her.

"Oh, John," she said. "I'm so sorry. Are you okay?"

"I am now. Now that I know you are, that I'm with you. You can never go back to him. Never."

"I'm not. I won't. I'm moving in with Mom until I can . . .

until things get . . ."

I nodded.

"I'm so worried," she said. "I have such a bad feeling. Larry's crazy. He's . . . He'll do . . . He's capable of anything. And if Bobby Battle told him about Raymond and Vincent, what else has he told him?"

"It'll be okay. We'll figure it out. I promise."

"I've fallen in love with you, John. Totally and completely. Head over heels. The real deal."

"I love you," I said. "I'm so in love with you."

"I've already contacted an attorney," she said. "I'm . . . I'll be free of him at last. For good. And then . . ."

"And then," I said. "I like the sound of that."

"Speaking of sounds," she said, "I know it's way too early . . . And we'll probably never live long enough to even . . . And I'm not sayin' you would even want to . . . even way out there in the future, but . . ."

"Yeah?"

"It'll show you where my mind is. Well . . . I've thought about it. I can't help myself. I did. And . . . I just . . . I can't be Jordan Jordan."

Frank Morgan called me the next morning.

I tripped over Martin, who was asleep on the floor, on my way over to the phone.

"Did I wake you?" Morgan asked.

"No. Not at all. How's it goin'?"

"I've got meetings this morning and I wanted a chance to talk to you before I got tied up."

"I appreciate you callin'."

"Only have a few minutes, so here it is . . . Ralph Alderman was forced to leave because of inappropriate behavior—some of it involving kids. The guy's not right. If somebody had done their damn job back then, he wouldn't be working around kids now."

I thought about it.

"I don't have a lot of details. It was all handled very quietly—not a lot written down. Force gave him the chance to resign and he took it. Became a mall cop. Had some complaints there too. Eventually was pushed out. Allowed to resign. Everybody just kicked the can down the road. No complaints filed at Safe Haven so far. He's had that job a while too. So . . . maybe there was nothin' to the other stuff or he's changed."

"Or he's gotten far better at it," I said.

"Could be," he said. "Probably is. Of the three it's the most likely. Sorry I don't have more . . . but . . . it's enough . . . to warrant a second look at him."

"Yes it is."

"What kind of man keeps company with kids?" he said.

I looked over at Martin.

This kind of man, I thought, and reminded myself not to jump too quickly to conclusions where Ralph or anyone else was concerned.

"There's a few other people we can talk to about him," he said. "Get more information—kind of stuff not in the file—but it'll take some time to track 'em down."

"Thank you," I said.

"Thank *you*. Wish I had you on all my cases."

That put a small lump in my throat and I was unable to respond.

"As for the other . . ." he began.

"The other?"

"Cases similar to LaMarcus's."

"Oh."

"So far no luck. I mean, we've got a few with similarities . . . but not enough in common to . . . I don't know. If this case had a list like the Atlanta Child Murders case did and LaMarcus was the pattern case . . . I don't think any of these would make it. We've got some killed with the same drug, the chloral hydrate stuff, but no real abductions and no rape."

"Okay," I said. "Thanks for looking."

"I've still got a few agents on it . . . so we'll see, but I think we're gettin' close to exhausting cases to examine."

"Any way I could take a look at the ones that had any similarities at all?"

"Sure."

"You sure?" I asked. "You don't mind?"

"I knew you would want to—and I know we need you to. Already made copies for you. Got a guy dropping 'em by the college later this morning."

"Thanks, Frank," I said. "Thank you so much. Before you go . . ."

"Yeah?"

"How well do you know Bobby Battle?" I asked.

"Tell me you don't suspect him."

I laughed. "I don't."

"Not all that well. But I think with him what you see is what you get. Why?"

"Would he tell Larry Moore about Jordan?"

"What about her, John?"

"About Ray and Vince and . . . He put her in the emergency room again. Told her he was going to find and kill Ray and Vince."

"He's the kind that would too. Crazy son of a bitch. I can't imagine Bobby would say anything to him, but I can't say for certain he didn't or wouldn't. I just don't know."

"How else would he know?"

"You want me to talk to Bobby?"

"I'll do it," I said.

"Tell you who you need to be talkin' to. Your dad. Have you?"

"Not yet."

"John."

"It's not for lack of effort on my part."

"Keep tryin'. You won't be sorry. I swear it."

"Thanks, Frank," I said. "I know. I know you're right. I'll do it today. I'll call him again today."

Chapter Forty-one

I was sitting at a table in an empty classroom at EPI, the case files Frank had copied for me spread out before me.

After my morning classes, I had gone upstairs and borrowed Randy Renfroe's phone and called Ida's home number to check on Jordan.

I let it ring several times, but no one ever picked up.

I began worrying about her immediately, my imagination inventing several scenarios, displaying them on the big screen of my mind in vivid detail, as I punched in the number for Safe Haven.

"Are you okay?" Randy asked.

I nodded. "Thanks."

Jordan answered the phone.

"Hey," I said. "What're you doin' there? Thought you were resting at Ida's?"

"I can't just sit there," she said. "They need my help here and it takes my mind off it."

"But you need to—"

"Larry came by."

"When? What'd he—"

"Thankfully, it was before Mom left, so she helped. We decided it was best I wasn't alone there."

"I'm glad you did. I wish I had—"

"John, be very careful. He was braggin' about what he had done and making threats about what he would do, saying he would finish takin' care of all our problems soon."

"What'd he brag about doin'?"

"Said the two faggots would never threaten his girl again. John, I'm scared."

As I looked through the files of children who went to sleep and never woke up, I thought about my conversation with Jordan and what to do about Larry.

What could I do?

The woman I loved was in real danger—hell, so was I—and what could I do about it? What could an ordinary citizen do about a cop? But I wasn't even an ordinary citizen. I was a broke college student in a new town, with no pull, no power, no connections, nothing that was of any use to Jordan or much use to anyone else.

I studied the files harder, trying to distance myself from the dread spreading outward from my core as if a poison plunged into my racing heart.

Concentrate. Focus.

I looked over Ralph's file first. Frank was right. There just wasn't much there.

Then I turned my attention to sleeping little angels.

The first few were ruled accidental overdose, which was what they appeared to be. Noctec prescribed for children with insomnia. Parents who would have to live with the fact that they had unwittingly killed their own child. In a couple of the cases, a parent had administered the drug not realizing the other parent already had. In a couple of others it was simply a case of too large a dosage. None of these involved abduction or rape. Nothing even suspicious.

Of the rest, all but two had an obvious suspect—whether convicted or even arrested or not.

That left two cases where, like LaMarcus's, there was no

clear motive or suspect, where the why and the who remained unknown.

Putting aside all other files but Ralph's and these two child murder cases, I dug in, examining every detail, going back and forth between them, comparing, contrasting, questioning, challenging.

Both cases involved little black boys near LaMarcus's age when he was murdered. Both were good kids from good homes. Both were killed at home, their bodies found on or near their property.

And then I saw it.

The first boy had spent the afternoon at South Dekalb mall with his friends on the day he died. He and his friends had even had a run-in with a mall security guard, Ralph Alderman, who had given a statement to the police. The officer who took the statement was Larry Moore.

The second boy, who was killed about a year later, attended Safe Haven Daycare and Aftercare Academy. He had been particularly close to the school's resource officer, a Ralph Alderman, who had stated during his interview what a fine young man the boy had been, what a tragedy this was, and how very much he'd be missed, especially by Alderman himself.

I rushed upstairs to call Jordan.

Pam's office was empty so I helped myself to her phone.

"What is it? Are you okay?" she asked.

"Do you remember a kid who came through there named Atwood Jones?"

"Mom and I spoke at his funeral. We've done more of that over the years than I care to remember, but his was more difficult than most. Wasn't sick. Didn't have an accident. It was so sudden. Shocking. I don't think they ever even figured out what he died of."

"They did," I said. "Same as LaMarcus."

"*What*? Really? Oh my God. Are you sure?"

"How close were he and Ralph?"

There was a long pause.

"Very. Oh, God, John. No. Please no."

"Is he there now?"

"He is."

"Okay. Just act normal. Everything's going to be okay. Keep an eye on him but be careful not to let him know you know anything."

"Okay."

"I love you."

"I love *you*."

I hung up, then lifted the receiver again and punched in Bobby Battle's number.

"I's just about to call you," he said. "Guess whose tickets got punched in an early mornin' shootout?"

"Ray and Vince?"

"Give that man a prize."

"What do I win if I guess who shot 'em?" I said.

"Wait just a minute now."

"It was Larry Moore, wasn't it?" I said. "You told him they had threatened his wife. You knew he would kill them."

"I never told him shit," he said. "Haven't spoken to the crazy bastard in a while—and then only in passing. I know maybe your head's a little messed up and you're under a lot of stress, but that's a very serious allegation you're makin'. And there's no truth in it. I swear. So do me a favor and just say thank you for callin' you with the good news."

"Thank you," I said.

We were quiet a beat while I wondered if I really believed him.

"Can you come to the college?" I said. "I've got some evidence you need to see."

"Sure, John," he said. "It's not like I'm doin' anything else."

"It's important."

"Lucky for you I was about to go to lunch," he said. "I'll

stop by on my way."

"Thank you," I said. "I mean it."

"Hell," he said, "I thought you meant it before."

When I got off the phone, Pam Palmer appeared in the doorway.

"Randy, Mr. Aycock, and I need to talk to you for a minute," she said.

"Can it wait? I'm in the middle of something really important."

"We'll try to make it as brief as possible."

We walked over to Pete Aycock's office and she closed the door behind us.

Pete Aycock, a trim, suave, self-possessed middle-aged man, was the president of the school. He was a calm, plain-spoken pragmatist, who often took time to talk with students, illustrating his many points with homespun stories and movie metaphors. Recently, he had used the hit movie *Top Gun* to point out to me the importance of being under authority and having a wingman.

"This is difficult," Randy said. "You're a great student and such a wonderful addition to our school and church. You're doing a good job with the facilities, and the ministry work you're doing in your covenant community is exemplary."

What the hell is so bad it requires that kind of buildup in front of the president of the college?

"You really are such an asset," Pam said. "Such an example of the kind of students we want EPI to attract."

"But?" I said. "What is it?"

"One of your fellow students said you've had a married woman in your dorm room at night."

"Oh."

"I really hope it's not true," Randy said. "Female guests are only allowed in the living room and never past midnight. But we would hope as a student at EPI and a minister in our church, you wouldn't have a married woman anywhere in the apartment."

"I understand," I said.

We were all silent a beat. Pete Aycock, who always wore a silk tie, pressed white shirt, and a conservative suit that looked tailored for him, recrossed his legs, swept away a piece of lint from his lapel with the backs of his fingers, straightened his tie, and cleared his throat.

"Is it true?" he asked.

"Is what true?"

"Are you sleeping with a married woman?" Pam said. "Having an affair? Bringing her into your room?"

"No. No. And yes. I'm not sleeping with or having an affair with anyone. But yes, a soon-to-be-divorced, technically still-married woman has been in my room. Never alone. Always with a neighbor kid, who's almost always there. Has anyone complained about him?"

Pam shook her head.

I nodded.

"Listen, John," Pete said, "just be smart. Okay? Being guileless is good, but you need to be wise too. What was it Jesus said? Be as innocent as a dove but as shrewd as a snake."

"It's best if all guests keep their visits confined to the living room," Randy said. "That's all we're saying. That's all. Follow the dorm rules. Avoid even the appearance of . . . impropriety."

Chapter Forty-two

When Battle arrived, I took him down to the classroom where I had the files spread out on the table.

"The fuck you doin' with these?" he said.

"Your job."

"I didn't come here to be insulted," he said, turning to leave. "I was doin' you a fuckin' favor."

"Sorry," I said. "I'm . . . I just feel . . . I'm sorry. I shouldn't've said it."

He turned back around. "You got five minutes."

It took less than four to lay out for him what I had.

"You son of a bitch," he said. "You fuckin' son of a bitch. That fits. That's . . . that really could be it."

It felt good to hear him say it.

"So, Alderman kills LaMarcus," he said. "We don't know if that's the first or if he had done it before, and since then . . . he's killed—but wouldn't there be more? Why only two?"

"Only two we found so far. I bet there are others."

"But LaMarcus's body was moved and raped. None of these others are."

"I've thought about that," I said. "Everything that's different from these other cases was done post-mortem. So either he didn't have opportunity with these once they were dead . . . or . . . LaMarcus was killed during the Atlanta Child Murders case period. So the killer tried to make it look like LaMarcus was part of that—after he was dead. Tied the rope around his neck, roughed up the body, tried to make it look like something it wasn't. Even the rape occurred after death. But what if it was staged too. What if he just put a condom on an object and inserted it to make it look like rape."

He was nodding. "Makes a certain sense."

"So we go talk to him?"

"What? No. We've got to build a case. I've got to talk to my captain. We've got to gather what we can find. See if there are other victims that we might be able to link to him. See if we can get enough for a judge to grant us a warrant. And after all that's done, see if the DA thinks we have enough for an arrest.

"Talkin' to him is the last thing we need to do right now—and the *we* I'm talkin' about is the Decatur Police Department. I appreciate what you've done. This is great shit. Really great. And it may even be the thing that breaks the case and leads to an arrest, but this is where things get very tricky. We have to follow proper procedure and protocol or the case can get tossed on a stupid technicality. This is very important. Don't fuck up a case you may very well have solved by doing anything stupid. Stay away from Alderman. Stay away from Safe Haven. Stop detecting. Understand?"

I nodded.

"I mean it."

"I know."

"Let me hear you say you will."

"I will."

"Good work, John. I mean it. Very good work."

I stood there thinking for a long while after he had gone.

I knew what he had said was true, knew it was how it had to be. What I didn't know was if I could be okay with it.

Could I sit back and do nothing? Be satisfied with the contribution I had made, occupy my mind with something else, go back to reinvestigating the Atlanta Child Murders? Or would it be so frustrating that I'd exist in a dark, angry place, thinking and drinking too much, experiencing peace and joy too little.

I'd have to figure it out, figure out what I wanted to do, who I wanted to be and become. Should I drop out of Bible college and study criminology, become a cop like Battle and Frank and my dad? Should I keep studying ministry and try to figure out a means and a milieu to bring these two disparate callings together? But what could that be?

Even if I became a cop, I'd reach a point in every case where I had to turn it over to others. The most I could hope for would be to take an investigation as far as it could go, make an arrest, look a killer in the eye, stand there and be a witness for his victim, then hand it over to others, others who make deals and plea bargains and lose cases on technicalities. Could I do that? Would that be any better than this? It would, because I could at least see a case through to its conclusion.

The classroom door jerked open and Bobby Battle walked back in.

"Guess we're not going to have to wait after all," he said. "There's a kid missin' from Safe Haven. Come on."

Chapter Forty-three

"Lord help me Jesus, it's happenin' again," Ida said.

She was panicking. She wasn't the only one.

We were standing on the walkway close to the entrance.

"I've got the school on lockdown," Ralph was saying to Bobby Battle. "Every child but the missing boy is inside the building and accounted for."

He was sweating profusely, wiping his brow often with his fat fingers, slinging the salty liquid off his hand onto the sidewalk.

"Here's a picture of him," Jordan said.

She passed out xeroxed copies of a young black boy who could be LaMarcus's brother.

"How long's he been missin'?" Battle asked.

Ida opened her mouth but nothing came out.

"We're not sure exactly," Jordan said. "But we can narrow it down some. The kids eat in the same place, at the same table with the same group every day, every time they eat. It's one of the ways we take count, keep tabs. We know Brandon was here at ten-fifteen for snack time. We know he was here at eleven when we did our last count before the lunch break. When we sat down at twelve-fifteen for lunch he was gone. We just don't know how long after eleven he was here."

"Okay," Battle said. "That helps. And the kid's name is Brandon?"

"Brandon Wright."

"And you've searched all the normal places?" he said. "All through the building, every room, every nook and cranny, every hiding spot on the playground and property?"

Ralph was nodding vigorously before Battle finished. "Everywhere. We wouldn't've called you if we hadn't. The boy is not on the premises."

"Who's been here?" Battle said.

Ralph handed him a sheet of paper. "I log everybody—parent, teacher, student, visitor—in and out on my log."

I glanced at it over his shoulder. There were only four names.

"This is everybody?"

He nodded.

"Who are they?"

"These two are parents. One dropped off her child late. The other picked his up for a dentist appointment. The other one was a delivery—food and kitchen supplies— and this last one was looking the place over, trying to decide whether or not to send his kid here."

"His?"

"Recently divorced single dad."

"What'd he drive? Got a phone number, description, anything?"

Ralph's eyes grew wide as he shook his head.

"Did he sign his kid up?" Battle asked Ida. "Leave any info?"

She shook her head.

"What about the food delivery person?" he asked. "Y'all know him?"

"Her, and yes. She's been doing it for several years now."

Two Dekalb County patrol cars pulled into the driveway.

"I don't want any panicking. Everybody calm down. I

want you to make sure the kids are okay, that they have no idea what is goin' on. Can you do that, while also asking if anybody knows where Brandon is or saw him leaving?"

Both Ida and Jordan nodded.

"Okay. Go do that. And do another search for him inside. We're gonna start looking around out here."

"Come on, Mom," Jordan said, and led her back to her home become daycare where this had happened before.

"I wanna head up the search," Ralph said. "I know this area better than anyone. And the kid. And this happened on my watch."

"You can help," Battle said. "Stick with me and John. But I also need you comin' up with a description and vehicle for the man who stopped by to check out the school."

The four cops from the two patrol cars joined us, and Battle explained the situation and divvied up the search assignments. "Let's find him," he said. "Alive."

As the officers headed in various directions, I said, "I want to start with LaMarcus's hideout. If he's not there, then the drainage culvert."

"Was thinkin' the same thing," Battle said.

"Oh my God," Ralph said. "Do y'all think . . . Please God no, not again."

Battle and I rushed to the backyard, Ralph following behind as best he could.

When we reached the spot where we had been reenacting LaMarcus's abduction just a few months before, we slowed just enough to keep from falling as we pressed in through the bushes and stepped inside the child's hideout become crime scene.

There was nothing there. No child. No body. No evidence. No sign anyone had been here since we were last.

Relief washed over me but only momentarily.

I took off for the drainage ditch and the culvert where

LaMarcus had been laid out, Battle beside me, Ralph falling farther and farther behind.

Rushing through the small wooded boundary at the back of the property, we jumped the fence and came out into Flat Shoals Estates.

Not waiting for Ralph, not sure if he could make it over the fence, we ran down the sidewalk, through the cul-de-sac, and into the woods beyond, no sign of Ralph as we did.

We stumbled down the slope, around the drainage area, over to the culvert, and looked inside.

It was empty.

Thank you. Thank you for that, I prayed as relief washed over me again.

"That's good," Battle said. "But what's it mean? Where can he be?"

We turned and walked back up the incline, through the woods, out the cul-de-sac, and up the sidewalk toward Safe Haven. There was still no sign of Ralph.

Chapter Forty-four

When we were in the backyard again, we walked over to the window and motioned for Jordan.

"Any sign of him?" Battle asked.

"No. We've searched the entire building again."

"How's everyone holding up?"

"The kids are fine. So are the other workers. Mom and I not so much. I can't believe this is happening to us again."

I reached up and took her hand, rubbing her fingers around her brace.

She looked down and tried to smile but when she did tears started coming.

"Do you mind callin' the two parents who picked up their kids?" I said. "Just feel them out. See if they know anything. See if maybe Brandon hitched a ride somehow."

She nodded.

"Where's Ralph?" Battle said.

"Haven't seen him lately. He's acting so . . . flakey today. I mean more so than usual. Do you think . . . He . . . He may be at his house. He was back and forth for some reason earlier."

"Shit," Battle said. "Come on."

I squeezed her fingers. "Hang in there," I said. "I love you." And then followed after him.

When we came around to the front, Frank Morgan was

pulling up and Ralph was standing at his guard stand at the front gate.

"Ralph," Battle yelled. "What the hell you doin'?"

"Couldn't keep up with you two," he said. "Didn't realize it was a race."

"Did you come up with anything on the visitor for me yet?" Battle said.

"Workin' on it now."

We walked over to Frank and filled him in.

"What can I do?" he said.

"Help us with this fat fuck right here," Battle said. "Your boy here thinks he might be the doer."

He nodded nonchalantly.

"No . . . *the* doer."

"Oh."

"Tell him," he said.

I did.

"Can't believe we missed that," he said.

Battle radioed the other officers for updates. No one had turned up anything yet. He told them to expand the search in every direction, including the Flat Shoals Estates subdivision.

"Which one is fat boy's house?" Battle asked me when he was off his radio.

"Right there."

He then turned and walked back over to where Ralph stood.

"Who lives there?" he asked.

"I do."

"You?"

"Yeah. Why?"

"We need to search it. Makes it a lot easier being yours. I had no idea. Toss me your keys and we'll check it out."

"I don't understand."

"What? What don't you understand?"

"Why you need to search my house. It's locked. He can't have gotten in."

"We've got to search everywhere. You know that. You used to be on the force, didn't you?"

"Yeah."

"Then you get it."

"Sure. Yeah. Come on. I'll take you over."

Battle motioned for me and Frank, and the three of us followed Ralph over to his house.

The small red brick house smelled of starch and mothballs and mildew. Mostly of mildew.

It was dirty and in disrepair, cluttered and not cared for, but more in an inept bachelor than a serial killer way. It was what you'd expect from an unhygienic overweight slob, which didn't mean he wasn't a serial killer.

"It's a mess, boys," he said. "Maid's day off. Wasn't expectin' company. Been workin' extra hours at Safe Haven."

"It's fine," Frank said. "Looks about like my place when company drops in unexpectedly."

We split up and searched the small house, which didn't take long. While doing so, I asked to use the bathroom and let water run in the sink while I rifled through the medicine cabinet, drawers beneath the counter, and small linen closet.

I found a pharmacy.

Most pills weren't in bottles. Most of the ones that were no longer bore a label.

When I walked out, Battle was saying, "What about the basement?"

"Can only be accessed from outside," Ralph said.

"Then let's go outside and access it."

As Ralph led the way and Battle followed, Frank and I took our time.

"Anything?" Frank asked.

"Everything," I said. "Never seen so many pills in one place before."

"If this is our guy, where's the body?"

"He could be the guy and have nothin' to do with Brandon being missing," I said. "Or he could've hid him somewhere other than his home."

By the time Frank and I reached the backyard, Ralph had a key in the padlock in the hasp on the cellar doors and was jiggling it, trying to get it open.

The once white doors were covered in green mold and black mildew and needed painting. They were on the back right side of the house and stood about four feet high.

"My key's not workin'," Ralph said. "It's been a while since I've been in here but I've never not had my key work."

"Got bolt cutters?" Battle said.

"In the basement. But hell, if I can't get in, no way a little boy did. You know?"

"Does the daycare?"

He nodded.

"I'll run grab 'em," I said. "Be right back."

I ran over to Safe Haven as fast as I could.

When I opened the door, Jordan rushed over to me.

"Find him?" she asked.

I shook my head. "Not yet. Anything here?"

She shook her head.

"I need bolt cutters. Ralph said there were some here."

She nodded. "Come with me."

She led me to what used to be the house's garage. It was filled with all manner of interior and exterior tools and supplies and equipment.

I found the bolt cutters on a shelf next to a couple of padlocks still in packages and one old one that had been cut, not far from an ax, sledgehammer, and hedge clippers.

As we were about to leave, I eased the door shut, took

Jordan in my arms and kissed her.

"God, I needed that," she said. "Thank you."

"More where that came from. Let's reconvene as soon as we can."

When I turned to open the door, she swatted my ass. "Such a great ass."

I rushed back over to Ralph's house with the bolt cutters and, though Ralph reached out for them, gave them to Battle.

"I'll buy you a new lock," he said to Ralph as the bolt cutters pinched one part of the metal lock bar in two.

As I removed the lock, Battle tossed the bolt cutters to the ground, and then we each grabbed one of the doors and yanked, and there on the ground was the curled-up body of Brandon Wright.

Chapter Forty-five

Frank and I ducked down into the basement as Battle tackled Ralph to the ground and cuffed him.

"He alive?" Battle yelled from behind us.

I couldn't tell yet if he was dead or just sleeping.

"IS HE ALIVE?" Battle yelled.

Frank felt for a pulse, moved his hand around to make sure, then shook his head.

I began to scoop up his small body to carry him out, but Frank stopped me. "Nothing we can do for him," he said. "It's a crime scene now. Let's slip out and preserve everything for the techs to process."

"Come on, you sick piece of shit," Battle was saying as he jerked Ralph to his feet.

"Why're you doin' this?" Ralph said. "I didn't put him in there. I'm . . . I didn't do anything."

Battle shoved him and he started stumbling back toward Safe Haven.

"We didn't make it in time," I said to Frank.

"We rarely do," he said. "We rarely ever do."

Battle then radioed the other officers, two of whom rushed over and grabbed Ralph's arms and ushered him toward their car.

"Guys, stop. Listen to me. I swear to God I didn't do it.

I swear. I have no idea who did that, who put him in my basement, but it wasn't me. Are you listening? LISTEN TO ME. I DIDN'T DO IT. Please, God, you've got to believe me."

"How many have there been?" Battle asked.

"What? None."

"Was LaMarcus the first?"

"*What*? No. God, no. I didn't kill LaMarcus. I haven't killed anybody. I swear. I would never. I could never. John, tell them. John? John, please."

As we reached Safe Haven and passed by the place where Ralph stood watch every day, something across the street caught my eye.

There, across Flat Shoals Road, in the driveway of a house on a hill, Larry Moore, in street clothes, sat in his black Trans Am, the window down, his feathered hair waving in the wind. Or maybe this last was my imagination.

I walked up to Ralph. "Was Larry Moore here this morning?"

He looked confused, then nodded.

"Why isn't he on the list?"

"He didn't go inside. Was just out front for a little while. John, I didn't do it. I swear. Please believe me. Please help me. Tell Miss Ida and Miss Jordan I'm sorry. Tell them I could never hurt anybody."

As Ralph was shoved into the backseat of the patrol car by the two cops, Larry cranked up his black sports car and slowly drifted down into the traffic on Flat Shoals and disappeared.

I rushed up the walkway toward the daycare center to tell Ida and Jordan, but before I reached it the door opened and they stepped out.

"You found him?"

I nodded. "In Ralph's basement."

"Jesus, no," Ida said.

“Is he okay?” Jordan said.

I shook my head. “We were too late.”

Both women began to cry, shaking as they fell into each other’s arms.

“I’m so sorry,” I said. “So, so sorry.”

Chapter Forty-six

"Still can't believe he did it," Ida said, tears still occasionally trickling down her dark cheeks. "Ralph."

It was later in the afternoon.

All the kids were gone.

All but a few of the workers released too.

GBI's crime scene division was working the entire area—Ralph's house, the daycare, the grounds, the neighborhood.

"All this time," she said. "I just can't . . ."

We were sitting by the front windows, Ida, Jordan, and I, in the art project area, watching all the police and forensic activity outside.

We each had coffee. None of us had touched it.

"Thinking back on it now," I said, "anything stand out about Ralph? Anything come to mind that didn't seem suspicious at the time but now seems . . ."

They both seemed to think about it for a long moment.

Eventually, Ida shook her head and Jordan said, "Nothing. I still can't believe he did it."

"Did Larry come by this morning?" I asked.

"Here?" Jordan said. "No."

Ida nodded. "He did too. Saw him out back. He came to talk to you—or stalk you or whatever the . . . I told him if he didn't leave I was calling the police."

"You saw him in the back?" I asked. "Just standing in the backyard?"

She nodded. "Why?"

"Ralph said he was in the front but didn't come in. I wonder if he drove around and parked in Flat Shoals Estates and walked in through the wooded area."

"He's done that before," Jordan said.

Ida shook her head. "He needs to be in custody too."

"Did y'all know Larry when LaMarcus was killed?"

"Not really know," Jordan said. "He used to come around with his dad some."

"His dad?"

"Did our yard," Ida said. "Handyman too. Helped out a lot after I lost . . . after *we* lost Jordan's dad. That's how they met. Can't believe Larry turned out the way he has."

"Did either of you see Ralph with Brandon this morning?"

They both shook their heads.

"Were they close?"

"Not particularly, no," Ida said.

"Ralph was awkward around all the kids," Jordan said. "But he tried to interact with them. Some more than others."

"Did he spend time with LaMarcus? Do you remember him being around?"

Ida shook her head.

We all fell silent a moment.

"Safe Haven," Ida said to herself, shaking her head. "No one will ever send their child back here. It's . . . over. I've . . . lost . . . everything."

"I'm so sorry," I said.

Jordan began to cry again.

"Should've never opened it in the first place," Ida added. "Not me. Not here. It's cursed. I'm cursed. Can't take care of my own child, gonna take care of other people's."

A cop came to the door. "Detective Battle said you can go, ma'am. He'll call or come by later."

Ida nodded absently.

"And he'd like to see you, sir," he said to me.

I nodded. "Thanks."

And then he was gone.

"Ralph never had kids of his own, did he?" I asked.

Ida shook her head.

"You ready to go, Mom?" Jordan asked, reaching over and rubbing her arm.

Ida shrugged.

"I'll get the car and pull up," she said. "You've done it enough times for me."

"Can you drive with your sling?" I asked.

She nodded. "I'm fine to drive. Thanks."

She then got up, gave me a kiss, and grabbed the keys from her mom's purse.

If Ida noticed the kiss, she gave no indication.

"Did Ralph have any nephews or nieces? Ever have any kids over?"

Ida shook her head.

"I'm just wondering way back when how he got a children's sleep aid."

Ida didn't respond, just continued staring out the window.

"Stole it?" Jordan offered with a shrug. "Black market? He was a cop back then. Could've gotten it anywhere. I'll be back in a minute, Mama."

"I'll walk her down when you pull up," I said.

"Thanks."

Jordan left and Ida and I were alone in the building.

"I'm just wondering how . . . Did LaMarcus take anything to help him sleep?" I asked.

She shook her head. "That boy never had no trouble sleepin'. Head hit the pillow, he out like a light. Now his sister on the other hand . . . that's a different story."

I looked through the window and watched as Jordan walked beneath the awning toward Ida's car, and everything suddenly fell into place.

My stomach lurched and I had a hard time not throwing up.

"Jordan had trouble sleeping?" I asked, wondering if Ida could hear how different my words sounded now.

She nodded. "Child never slept. Had to take something for the little bit she did get."

"Do you remember what she took?"

"Some stuff . . . Nordic or somethin'."

"Noctec?"

"That's it," she said.

"Yes it is," I said.

I helped her up and we began making our way toward the door.

"Did you say at group the other day that LaMarcus had some health issues?"

"Poor thing," she said. "Struggled with his little system, his tummy and . . . Jordan took such good care of him, was such a good big sister to her new little black brother."

We walked out the door and started down the walkway, me finding it difficult to put one foot in front of the other.

I felt dead inside, felt as if I couldn't feel, felt distant, as if everything including my self was a great ways away, up out of the deep, dark well I had fallen into.

"And her daughter . . . Savannah . . ." I said. "Jordan said she was sickly."

"All her little life," she said.

"What did she die of?"

"SIDS. My poor, poor girl," she said, as Jordan pulled up in the car. "She's been through so much. Too much. She's the sweetest, best thing God ever created and . . . she's suffered so much."

"I need to ask you one more thing," I said. "I've been meaning to and just haven't gotten to it yet."

"What is it, son?"

"Just something I'm not clear about. When LaMarcus went missing . . . why didn't you check his hideout? I would've thought that was the first place you'd look."

"I did. Well, I didn't. I was on the phone to the police, but it's the first place I sent Jordan. The very first."

Chapter Forty-seven

"Are you okay?" Jordan asked. "You're pale as a ghost."

I nodded.

I had just helped Ida into the passenger side of the car and felt like I was going to fall over.

"You sure? You really don't look good. All clammy and—"

"Just tired."

"Come over when you finish here. We need you. We'll take care of you too. Okay?"

I nodded and closed the door.

I could hear her saying "I love you" as the door closed.

After they were gone, I stepped over to Bobby Battle.

"You got Ralph's keys?" I asked him.

"Yeah. Why? I was just about to head back over to his house."

He tossed me a plastic evidence bag with the keys in them.

"I'll catch up with you," I said. "Wanna check something first."

On unsteady legs I walked back up to the converted house, out to the garage, and tried Ralph's cellar door key in the lock on the shelf next to where the bolt cutters had been.

It opened the lock.

Jordan had cut the lock and replaced it with another when she put Brandon's body inside Ralph's basement.

I collapsed to the cement floor and watched on the screen of my mind a very disturbed girl who made her little brother sick, who bribed him—probably with a Christmas gift she was wrapping—to hide in his hideout, who used her own sleeping medication on him, who moved the body and tried to make it look like he was a victim of the Atlanta Child Murderer—to garner even more sadness and sympathy, going as far as to stage strangulation and rape. A victim who married an abuser to get more sympathy. A deranged young woman who made her own child sick and then killed her. A murderer who went on to kill other children in her care, who mourned with their families and spoke at their funerals.

I thought about how eloquently she spoke about loss and grief to the support group, how at home she was in the center of the circle of concern and care for her, this poor, poor thing who had lost so much, who had so little left, who was so brave and strong, so good and kind.

I thought about how she had kept me away from Ida, asking to become the go-between, controlling the information, controlling everything. I wondered what secret Carlton had really told her, what else he had said that incriminated her.

Simple Larry never knew what hit him. He was her victim. Not the other way around. She had told him about Ray and Vince, not Bobby Battle.

And today she had set up Ralph, her readymade patsy, to take the fall. She had cut the lock, planted one of her victims to make another.

Pushing myself up, I went back inside the daycare and called Ida's house.

There was no answer.

Wondering where they could've gone, I called the church and asked for Pastor George Clarke, the parental grief group facilitator.

Ten minutes later I was meeting with him in his office.

Before becoming a pastor, this tall, soft-spoken African-American gentleman was a psychologist with a large private practice in Decatur.

Without telling him any names or divulging any information I didn't have to, I set up a hypothetical scenario and asked for his assessment.

"It's MSBP," he said. "Munchausen syndrome by proxy. A behavior pattern where a caregiver exaggerates, fabricates, or actually induces health problems—physical, psychological, behavioral, or mental—in someone under their care, most often a child. Munchausen syndrome is when someone does this to him or herself. By proxy is when it is done to someone in their power."

"Can someone suffer from both?" I asked.

He nodded. "I would think so. They are very similar. The way the by proxy form of it works is an adult caregiver, most often the mother, makes a child appear sick or actually makes the child sick in order to gain the attention, affection, sympathy of others—family, friends, doctors, nurses, strangers. Sometimes it's just fabrication and exaggeration, but others it actually involves purposely harming the child—often by poisoning, suffocation, or injection."

He paused. I nodded. He continued.

"This is one of the more misunderstood forms of child abuse and the most difficult to determine and deal with. The person suffering from this condition is a master manipulator, skilled at duplicity—the entire thing is based on deception."

Chapter Forty-eight

When I left the church, I didn't return to the crime scene, but instead drove straight to Ida's.

Both Battle and Frank had paged me several times and continued to.

I didn't care.

I knew I should take what little evidence I had to them.

I didn't care.

I knew the best chance for a conviction was to get them involved now and wait for them to build a case.

I didn't care.

She had let me fall in love with her. She had used me and manipulated me and made a fool of me.

I couldn't wait to confront her. It had to be now. It had to be me looking into her eyes. Right now nothing else mattered. Nothing else in the world.

When I reached Ida's, Larry's Trans Am was in the driveway next to her car.

I didn't care.

He and Ida could hear what I had to say together.

When I reached the front door, I found it ajar, the frame and molding around it splintered and broken.

Easing it open, I entered a bad situation and was about to make it worse.

Inside, I found the three of them in the living room, Larry with a weapon pointed at Jordan's head, Ida nearby pleading with him.

"The fuck do you think you're doin'?" Larry said when he saw me.

Ignoring him, I locked eyes with Jordan. "I know," I said.

"You know what?" Larry said.

Jordan frowned and nodded, tears starting to stream down her cheeks.

"She's leaving with me," Larry said. "You can wave bye or stay there and die. Up to you."

"How many kids have you killed?"

"I ain't killed any kids, retard," he said.

"Wasn't talkin' to you."

"The fuck this nut talkin' about?" he asked Jordan.

"She killed her little brother," I said. "After makin' him sick. She did the same to your child. And other children at Safe Haven, including Brandon Wright today."

"John," Ida said. "What're you . . . Ralph's the killer."

"Ralph's the fall guy," I said. "For a very sick girl with Munchausen syndrome by proxy."

"I've heard of that," Larry said.

Ever the victim, Jordan had yet to do anything but stand there crestfallen and cry.

How could I have fallen in love with her? How was it possible to be so imperceptive? What kind of detective was I that I could be so deceived? What kind of minister was I that I could become so intimate with evil and not know it?

"John, you can't think . . ." Ida began, but stopped, and seemed to look at Jordan as if for the first time, as if a not entirely unexpected dawning was taking place.

"It's when you make your kid sick for attention," Larry said. "You can't think that of—"

"I don't think it. I know it. And so do both of you," I said.

Neither of them said anything. Both of them seemed to consider it.

"How could you possibly think that of this poor, sweet, precious girl?" Ida said.

I told her. In detail. Everything I knew, everything I thought, everything I guessed, Larry listening intently as I did, eventually nodding as the unwitting witness to the truth.

"Think about it," I added. "There's no other way LaMarcus could've been taken from his own backyard with you watching him so closely. Had to be the other person who was supposed to be watching him, had to be a plan she came up with to make her brother an accomplice in his own murder."

Without realizing what I was doing until I had done it, I turned and looked over at the partially wrapped Christmas presents, the Star Wars lunchbox and Star Trek Communicators and other wrapped packages, gifts never given, reminders of innocents who never made it to Christmas, who would never see another Christmas again.

Ida followed my gaze, turning from me, to the presents, then to Jordan. "Baby, please tell me this isn't true. Please make it so I can't possibly believe this."

Jordan didn't say anything.

"Tell me you didn't torture and kill our little girl," Larry said. "Tell me you're not that kind of monster."

"I . . ." Jordan began. "I . . . need . . . treatment. It's . . . it's not me. It's . . . a disease. I don't want to be like . . . like . . . I don't want to have the affliction I have."

"*Affliction*?" Larry said. "No. No. No. It can't be. No. Please, God, no. Tell me you didn't do it. TELL ME."

Ida fell to the floor and began sobbing.

"Bitch, tell me you didn't kill my little girl," Larry demanded, jamming the barrel of his pistol into her forehead.

She didn't flinch. Just stood there, eyes downcast.

Eventually, she looked up at me, her eyes once again finding and focusing on mine.

"I'm so sorry, John," she said. "I really and truly fell in love with you. I so wanted us to be a family together."

"*Love*?" Larry said.

"Oh my God," Ida said. "Jordan, why did we go by John's? Jordan. What did you do to that little boy?"

Everything stopped.

"What did you do?" I said.

"I wanted . . . us . . . to . . . share . . . this."

"Jordan, no," I said. "Not Martin. Please. Not Martin too."

"You love him?" Larry said. "Look at me, you child-murdering faithless whore. Look at me."

She never looked at him. Not when he yelled for her to. Not when he thumbed back the hammer. Not when he shot her in the head before doing the same to himself.

Chapter Forty-nine

Martin was lying on my bed, his small body on its side in a fetal position.

So sweet, so innocent, so peaceful.

I made my way across the quiet room.

To be, or not to be, that is the question—

Was he sleeping, lost in the sweet dreams of the underworld or . . .

I strained to hear his breathing but could not.

To sleep—

I eased down on the bed beside him, sitting on the edge, not yet willing to know what once known I would never be able to unknow.

Perchance to Dream—

"Martin," I whispered.

So still. So quiet.

Aye, there's the rub—

"Martin?"

No response.

His weight on the bed was different somehow, as if the soul is something substantial, something palpable, something measurable.

For in that sleep of death, what dreams may come—

"Martin," I said again, this time a little louder.

The increased volume revealed a shaky, unsure quality in my voice. I sounded like a child in the darkness, filled with fear and dread, asking "Who's there?"

"Martin?" I said again. "Are you asleep?"

To die, to sleep no more—

I reached for him, but stopped just shy of touching him, just shy of confirming what I had known since Ida's pitiful, "Oh my God. Jordan, why did we go by John's? Jordan. What did you do to that little boy?"

"Martin, please," I said.

If it weren't for me, if I hadn't come into his life, if I hadn't brought one of the real monsters of childhood into his little life . . .

And by a sleep, to say we end the heart-ache, and the thousand natural shocks that flesh is heir to—

Finally, I summoned everything within me and closed the small distance between where my hand hung trembling to where the face of the sweet boy who called me Yon rested.

His flesh was cold.

For in that sleep of death, what dreams may come when we have shuffled off this mortal coil—

If I hadn't come into his life, if I hadn't brought Jordan . . .

"I'm so sorry," I said. "Martin, I'm so, so sorry."

I had come to Atlanta to find and stop a child killer. Instead, I had become an accessory to one. I hadn't just looked into Nietzsche's abyss. I had dived into it. And I had pulled little Martin Fisher into it with me.

I would never get over this. Not ever. Maybe Shakespeare was wrong. Maybe it wasn't death so much as regret and guilt and grief that was the real undiscovered country from whose bourn no traveler returned.

I would not return from this.

I would spend the rest of my life trying but never quite being able to fully return from this. I would try to help others return, try to prevent others from taking the journey at all, but there was no amount of good I could do, no amount of booze I could consume, no amount of justice I could administer to ever be enough to return from this dark country I was just beginning to discover.

Chapter Fifty

A cold numbness invaded my core and stayed there.

I was as detached as I had ever been, experiencing everything as if from a great distance away, becoming disinterested observer rather than participant in my own life.

I wasn't just depressed. I was devastated. Ironically, I didn't drink. I was beyond depressed, beyond devastated, beyond drink.

I didn't eat much of anything, but what I did had no taste whatsoever.

Frank Morgan and Bobby Battle both reached out to me, but I couldn't face them. I couldn't face anyone.

After several days of not leaving the apartment and of barely leaving my room, I ventured outside for the first time on a rainy Thursday morning.

The moment I stepped outside my door, my eyes, against my will, moved over to the basketball court. It was empty, but I could see Martin working on his shot, hear the echo of his small, singular voice.

I blinked back the tears threatening to join the misty raindrops swirling about my face.

I knew enough to know that it was probably temporary, but at the moment I honestly couldn't imagine ever playing basketball again.

I stumbled to my car, which after sitting five days I wasn't sure would crank, and drove out toward Ellenwood to Fairview Memorial Gardens.

Driving, like all my actions, felt foreign and odd, as if I was removed a certain distance from doing it.

During the drive out the day grew darker, but the reticent rain remained the same.

Jordan's plot wasn't far from a stone statue of Saint Mark, the bearded and robed apostle holding a tablet in his left hand, below him a lion lying at his feet.

As I approached the graveside, Ralph Alderman stepped away from where he was standing beside Ida and met me as I neared, blocking my entry to the modest memorial service taking place behind him.

He poked out his chest and expanded his elephantine girth and said, "You're not welcome here."

"Yes he is," Ida said from behind him. "Let him through."

He begrudgingly stepped aside and I walked past him. Ducking down beneath her umbrella, I hugged Ida.

There were only four people present—Pastor Don, Ida, Ralph, and myself. We stood around the small headstone with the bronze plate engraved with the name of the woman, the murderess, I had fallen in love with, who some part of me was still in love with.

We were standing in a sparse garden of fake flowers, dotted occasionally by a small tree or shrub.

I was the only one without an umbrella. It wasn't raining hard. I wouldn't have cared if it had been.

Pastor Don began with a prayer.

Ida wasn't crying. No one was.

After reading a few passages of scripture and a poem,

Pastor Don delivered an eloquent eulogy, prayed again, his words compassionate and comforting, then committed her soul to God and her body to the ground. Ashes to ashes. Dust to dust.

And then it was over.

Eventually, Ida and I were alone with Jordan.

In the silence between us I could hear all that couldn't be said. In the distance, the low rumble of thunder barely registered. Not far from where we stood, an American flag on a tall pole snapped smartly in the whining wind, its rigging clanging loudly.

"Got nothin' to say," she said at last.

I nodded.

"Well . . . just . . . that I won't ever get over this."

"Me either," I said.

It came out so softly, the wind taking it away so quickly, I wasn't sure she heard it. I didn't think it mattered either way.

"You loved her," she said.

"I did. Part of me still does. Probably always will."

We stood there for a few moments more, the rain and wind picking up a bit, large drops pelting my head with dull wet thumps I barely noticed. I was soon soaked through, hair dripping, clothes soggy.

"Nope," she said, "got nothin' else to say."

"Me either," I said. "Except . . . to say . . . I'm sorry."

She nodded. "Me too."

She turned to walk away. I stayed behind.

She had only taken a few steps when I turned to stop her.

"Sorry," I said, "but I need to . . . have to ask . . . Do you wish I hadn't . . . looked into . . . Would you rather I not have found out who . . . that it was her?"

She stood still for such a long moment I thought she wasn't going to answer. "Always better to know. Always. No matter the . . . cost."

She then turned and walked away and I was utterly and completely alone, the half-living among the full-dead, mourning the small, sweet, pretty monster who had done far more damage to me than if she had put me to sleep, for in this waking sleep of living death, what nightmares may come?

I have no idea how long I stood there alone, but eventually I wasn't alone any longer. Seeming to simply appear out of nowhere, Frank Morgan was suddenly standing beside me.

Like me, he had no umbrella. Like me, he was soaked through—so I knew he had been waiting a while. Like me, he said nothing.

We stood there like that, raindrops wetly thumping us, the soggy ground, and Jordan's headstone, the American flag flapping in the breeze, an unseen mourner crying for someone unknown to us close enough to be heard, neither of us uttering a sound.

We stood as stonily still and silent as Saint Mark beside us, and we stood that way for a very long time.

I don't know how long we stood there that way. I only know that during the entirety of our time together there, Frank never said a single word. There was nothing to say and he knew it. What he probably didn't know, what he couldn't possibly have known, was how much his silent presence meant to me, did for me. It was as healing as anything that had happened since I had lost everything—my surrogate wife and son, my joy, my confidence, my calling, my way entire—and I would never forget it or him or our random Thursday in the rain.

Leave a Review
Sign up for Michael's Newsletter
Get a FREE Book!

Thank you for reading INNOCENT BLOOD!

Please take a moment and write and post a review of it now.

Be sure to visit www.MichaelLister.com for more about other John Jordan Mysteries and Michael's other exciting novels.

Sign up for Michael's newsletter at www.MichaelLister.com and receive a free book!

About the Author

Multi-award-winning novelist Michael Lister is a native Floridian best known for literary suspense thrillers and mysteries.

The Florida Book Review says that "Vintage Michael Lister is poetic prose, exquisitely set scenes, characters who are damaged and faulty," and Michael Koryta says, "If you like crime writing with depth, suspense, and sterling prose, you should be reading Michael Lister," while *Publisher's Weekly* adds, "Lister's hard-edged prose ranks with the best of contemporary noir fiction."

Michael grew up in North Florida near the Gulf of Mexico and the Apalachicola River in a small town world famous for tupelo honey.

Truly a regional writer, North Florida is his beat.

In the early 90s, Michael became the youngest chaplain within the Florida Department of Corrections. For nearly a decade, he served as a contract, staff, then senior chaplain at three different facilities in the panhandle of Florida—a unique experience that led to his first novel, 1997's critically acclaimed POWER IN THE BLOOD. It was the first in a series of popular and celebrated novels featuring ex-cop turned prison chaplain John Jordan. Of the John Jordan series, Michael Connelly says, "Michael Lister may be the author of the most unique series running in mystery fiction. It crackles with tension and authenticity," while Julia Spencer-Fleming adds, "Michael Lister writes one of the most ambitious and unusual crime fiction series going. See what crime fiction is capable of."

Michael also writes historical hard-boiled thrillers, such as THE BIG GOODBYE, THE BIG BEYOND, and THE BIG HELLO featuring Jimmy "Soldier" Riley, a PI in Panama City during World War II (www.SoldierMysteries.com). Ace Atkins calls the "Soldier" series "tough and violent with snappy dialogue and great atmosphere . . . a suspenseful, romantic and historic ride."

Michael Lister won his first Florida Book Award for his literary novel DOUBLE EXPOSURE. His second Florida Book Award was for his fifth John Jordan novel BLOOD SACRIFICE.

Michael also writes popular and highly praised columns on film and art and meaning and life which can be found at www.MichaelListercom.

His nonfiction books include the "Meaning" series: THE MEANING OF LIFE, MEANING EVERY MOMENT, and THE MEANING OF LIFE IN MOVIES.

Lister's latest literary thrillers include DOUBLE EXPOSURE, THUNDER BEACH, BURNT OFFERINGS, SEPARATION ANXIETY, and A CERTAIN RETRIBUTION.

CPSIA information can be obtained at www.ICGtesting.com
Printed in the USA
LVOW10s1732091015

457650LV00006B/489/P